"I think Dee's looking for you," I said to Caitlen, looking over her shoulder toward the door.

As she turned around to see, I grabbed two of the longest french fries on my tray, dipped them heavily in ketchup, and shoved them up my nose.

"I don't see—" she started to say. But then she looked at me, looked at the french fries hanging out of my nose with ketchup dripping from the ends, and looked like she wanted to throw up.

Drool and Ed came running over. "That was fantastic, Iggy," Drool said. He grabbed two fries, dunked them in ketchup, and shoved them in his ears. "Try this one next time."

Books by M. M. Ragz

Eyeballs for Breakfast
Eyeballs for Lunch
French Fries Up Your Nose
Sewer Soup
Stiff Competition

Available from MINSTREL Books

FRENCH FRIES UP YOUR NOSE

M.M. RAGZ

A MINSTREL® BOOK

PUBLISHED BY POCKET BOOKS

New York   London   Toronto   Sydney   Tokyo   Singapore

This book is a work of fiction. Names, characters, places, and incidents either are products of the author's imagination or are used fictitiously. Any resemblance to actual events or locales or persons, living or dead, is entirely coincidental.

A MINSTREL PAPERBACK *ORIGINAL*

 A Minstrel Book published by
POCKET BOOKS, a division of Simon & Schuster Inc.
1230 Avenue of the Americas, New York, NY 10020

ISBN: 0-671-88410-7

First Minstrel Books printing February 1994

10 9 8 7 6 5 4 3 2 1

A MINSTREL BOOK and colophon are registered trademarks of Simon & Schuster Inc.

Cover art by Chuck Pyle

Printed in the U.S.A.

Dedicated to
Patricia MacDonald

With special thanks to

Jeanine Fazio
Jonathan Swerdlick

CHAPTER

1

I stood in the shadows at the back of our school auditorium. Mrs. Phister, my teacher, came over and stood next to me. She was looking straight ahead, keeping her eagle eyes open for trouble, but when she opened her mouth, I knew she was talking to me.

"Well, Mr. Sands," she said. "Are we waiting for a special invitation? Or are we planning to hang around back here for the whole assembly?"

The best answer to a question like that was no answer. I pretended to be busy looking around.

When she turned and stood in front of me, hands on hips, I knew she meant business. "Iggy Sands, I don't want to have to speak to you again. Dr. Harder wants to begin the assembly. Seats are not assigned today, but I don't want you hanging around back here. Find a seat."

I flashed her a big smile—lots of teeth—and saluted sharply. "Yes, ma'am. Whatever you say." But I picked up my book bag and hurried away from her. I didn't want to get thrown out—that would spoil everything.

I strolled down a side aisle and picked a seat in the middle of an empty row. As I sat down, I noticed that kids started to fill in the row on both sides of me. But they left the seats next to me empty. Good. I didn't want anyone too close.

I shoved my book bag down between my feet, put my head back, and closed my eyes. School—what a waste! I spent more time doing math problems that never came out right, underlining subjects and verbs, studying junk like the Pilgrims. Who cared if they spent months on a dinky ship coming to America? They should have stayed in England and minded their own business.

Suddenly I heard someone yell, "Hey, Iggy. You got a seat saved for me?" I opened my eyes and saw Drew Haygood pushing his way past the kids who were sitting in my row. They yelled and shoved at him as he crunched on their toes, stumbled over their knees, and finally plopped his body in the empty seat next to me.

Having Drew for a friend was like having a Saint Bernard around. The worst thing was the way he ate, and he was always hungry. Nothing ever made it completely into his mouth, and he usually had something dribbling down his chin. That's how he got his nickname—Drool. And no one, except for a few teachers and his parents, ever called him Drew.

As the lights started to go down, Drool leaned over to me and whispered loudly, "You set something up,

2

Iggy?" His breath hit like a wave of old tuna fish, and I felt a spray. I almost got up and moved, but I had only two friends I could trust in the whole world, and it just so happened that Drool was one of them.

He gave me a little shove. "Come on, Iggy. Tell me. You going to do something? Huh? And where's Ed? How come he's not here? Is he helping? Is he?"

I put my hand on his arm to try to quiet him down. I was wishing I had a cork big enough for his mouth.

As Dr. Harder, our principal, walked onstage, Drool leaned so close that his chin was practically resting on my shoulder. "You don't have to tell me what it is," he whispered. "I just want to know if I should be expecting something to happen. You don't have to say a word. Just nod."

I could feel my ear getting wet. I used my elbow to shove Drool away from me, and as I did, I caught the look on his face, like one of those puppies in the pet shop wanting someone to take him home. I patted his arm, looked at him, and let the corners of my mouth go up just a little. Then I nodded.

"Oh, boy, oh, boy," he said and was about to ask another question, but the microphone squealed and Dr. Harder began speaking. I squeezed Drool's arm to keep him from talking. Then I settled into my seat.

"Boys and girls," she said. "We have called this assembly to discuss the election of the Westford student council president for next year. As you all know, every spring three candidates are nominated and run a campaign, and the school votes for the person they feel will be the best leader. In the fall we will elect the other officers with the help of the president."

Drool leaned toward me again. In a loud whisper he said, "You'd be a great leader, Iggy." I wiped my ear and ignored him. I tried to ignore Dr. Harder, too, but I couldn't stop listening.

"If you are interested in having your name on the ballot," she said, "you must present a petition with sixty student signatures and a letter of recommendation from a teacher. The first three students who fulfill these requirements will then begin their campaigns. We are looking for students who are dedicated to Westford and are willing to work hard."

Well, that left me out.

But I started thinking. Student council president. What a school I'd run. We'd have recess and gym all day long. And field trips to rock concerts or the circus—forget stuffy, smelly museums. And we'd get rid of that disgusting food in the cafeteria. I'd have it catered instead, from good restaurants, like the Burger Factory or Taco Tasty.

Dr. Harder's voice interrupted my dream. "And now, a few of your teachers would like to talk to you about the meaning of voting and responsibility. We'll hear from Mr. Humphrey, our music teacher, first."

I tried not to listen to his whiny voice. I tried to get back my dreams of being president. But it wasn't working. It hit me like a bucket of cold water: No one would vote for me. I could count my friends on one hand and still have a few fingers left over. Besides, only nerds and freaks were on the student council.

Mr. Humphrey started to ramble. I started to get bored. It was time.

I bent over and unzipped my book bag. I felt through the stuff—the plastic vomit, the giant-size jar of Vaseline, the containers of tacks and stink bombs and rubber cement, the hand shockers, the pepper gum, and the fake spiders. Way at the bottom I found what I was looking for—a small remote control box.

Straightening up, I could feel Drool watching me, squirming, trying to get a look.

Mr. Humphrey's voice dragged on, like a record at the wrong speed. ". . . and with leadership comes . . ."

I flipped a switch on the box, and a small red light glowed.

". . . and only when we . . ."

I turned a knob, and the red light turned yellow.

Drool was practically jumping up and down in his seat, and I knew some of the kids around me were watching out of the corners of their eyes. But I knew they wouldn't dare say anything—not if they wanted to be around tomorrow.

". . . and with the election of a president . . ."

A final push of a button changed the light to green, and a furry gray creature about the size of my shoe raced right across the front of the stage and disappeared. Dead silence followed for about four seconds.

Then two girls in the front row screamed.

The animal dashed across the stage a second time.

More girls screamed.

And then, right on schedule, good old Ed jumped up from his seat down front and yelled, "They're rats. The school's being invaded by giant rats. Run!"

5

The shrieks got louder as the fuzz ball scampered onto the stage again, stopped, spun around, and disappeared into the side curtains.

Within minutes the place was wild. Some kids were running up the aisles. Others had jumped up on the seats. Teachers were scurrying around, but I couldn't tell if they were trying to get the kids under control or get out of there themselves.

Dr. Harder grabbed the mike from Mr. Humphrey and practically shouted, "Everyone is dismissed. Go back to class. There is no need for panic." Then she turned to Mr. Humphrey and said, "And for heaven's sake, call the custodians."

I sat there, watching everyone race for the exits.

Drool was standing over me, talking nonstop, spluttering and spraying. "Superfantastic. Spectacular. You're an electronic genius. You're the best."

I shoved the remote back into my bag, zipped it up, and handed it to Drool. As we walked out of the auditorium, I noticed a couple of kids watching me. Then they started to poke each other and whisper. I hated to admit it, but I kind of enjoyed being a celebrity.

CHAPTER
2

When the end of the day rolled around and no one had asked me about the rat, I left school feeling pretty good. Another successful day in the life of Iggy Sands.

I was rushing out after school to meet Ed when, coming around a corner, I ran into Murphy Darinzo— and I mean ran into him. The books he was carrying crashed to the floor, and papers scattered all over the place. Usually, I would have just kept going, but I liked Murphy. He was a smart kid, but he was okay— the kind that didn't mind helping out with homework once in a while.

As I bent down to pick up one of his books, he snatched it from my hand and said, "Don't bother."

I looked at him, surprised. "What's *your* problem?"

"You, Iggy. You're my problem. At least you were. But no more. Just stay away from me from now on, that's all."

7

I figured he was feeling grouchy because his papers were in a mess. "Let me give you a hand," I said, putting my book bag down and reaching for a paper.

Again he snatched it away. He stood up and looked down at me. "That stupid shaving cream stunt you pulled last week wasn't funny, you know. Michael and I spent days doing that project, and it's going to take us days to do it again."

"It wasn't my fault," I said.

"What do you mean, *it wasn't your fault?*" His voice was getting louder and a couple of kids had stopped to see what was going on. *"You're* the one who planted that shaving cream bomb in Michael's book bag. Everything in there—including our project—was a soggy mess."

"Then blame your friend Michael," I said. "He was asking for it. He was being a real pain in gym just because he was kickball captain. I decided to teach him a little lesson." I tried to keep my voice sounding casual. I didn't want to fight with Murphy.

"It was a lousy decision," Murphy said, his cheeks getting red. "Most of the time I can ignore your little jokes, but this time you went too far."

"So what do you want me to do? Say I'm sorry?"

He folded his arms across his chest. "That would be a start."

I looked around. About half a dozen kids were standing around, watching and listening. Apologize? Me? Iggy Sands? In front of all those people? "You know what, Murphy?" I asked, picking up my book bag. "You should work on that sense of humor of yours." And I started to walk away.

"Just don't expect anything from me, Iggy!" he shouted after me. "At least not until you're ready to apologize."

"Don't hold your breath!" I hollered back.

"Sometimes you're a jerk, Iggy Sands. A real jerk!"

Not many people can call me a jerk and get away with it. But I was already late meeting Ed, so I decided to pretend I didn't hear him.

Ed was waiting for me on the playground. "You got it?" I asked.

He handed me a wrinkled brown lunch bag. I reached into it and pulled out the mechanical rat. Checking for damage, I asked, "Did you have any trouble finding it?"

"Nope. It was right where you said it would be—behind the curtain on the left side of the stage. I shoved it into my book bag and was about to leave when Dr. Harder caught me up there."

"What did you tell her?"

Ed laughed. "I acted confused and scared and said I was lost."

"And she believed you?"

"Yup. I should have been an actor. She was so concerned about me that she walked me back to class."

That made me raise an eyebrow. "And you're sure she didn't suspect anything?"

"I told you—no."

"Well, just be careful when you're dealing with her. She's no dope, you know. Come on, let's get going. My dad's taking me out for pizza tonight and maybe a movie."

* * *

When I got home, I expected the house to be dark and empty like it was every afternoon, but when I opened the door, I could hear voices. The suitcase standing in the front hall gave me another clue that something was up.

My dad and I lived alone in a big old house on the outskirts of town. My mother left when I was only a baby, so I didn't remember anything about her. But I liked living alone with my father. He didn't lay down a lot of rules and he wasn't fussy. He used to talk about moving to a smaller place, but he just closed off the upstairs instead. I had my own room next to the kitchen, which was handy if I needed a midnight snack. I knew he worried about me sometimes— whether he was doing a good job as a parent. That's why I was careful never to get into any big trouble.

Just then, Dad came from the kitchen dressed in his black suit and white tie. "You're home from school pretty late, Iggy," he said.

"And you're kind of early," I said. "What's going on?"

Suddenly I heard pots and pans banging in the kitchen and someone whistling—very loud and very off-key. It could be only one person—Dottie Dumpler, a whopper of a woman who called herself a child care specialist. In other words, she was a baby-sitter.

"Dad, why's the Dumpster here?" I asked, feeling a slight panic in my voice. "Where are you going?"

"To a magicians' convention in Buffalo. My plane leaves in an hour."

"How come you didn't tell me?"

"I didn't know. Mr. Gross just told me today. He

10

was supposed to go, but he got a call—some kind of family emergency—and he asked me to cover for him. He pays my salary, so how could I refuse?"

"But what about our pizza night? And the movies?"

He reached into the closet and pulled out his trench coat. "As soon as I get back, we'll pig out on pizza every night until you're sick of it."

"But it's not fair."

"I know," he said. "And I'm sorry. But I brought you something." He reached into his inside pocket and started to pull out a bright red scarf. It kept coming and coming—first red, then blue, then green, and finally black. I watched as he made some quick movements with his fingers and *zingo*—there was a silk bouquet of flowers in a rainbow of colors. Before Dad got his job as manager of Gross's Magic Emporium, he used to be a magician. I think he did kids' parties and that kind of stuff. He still liked to fool around with it once in a while.

He handed the flowers to me and said, "It was defective. A customer returned it because the flowers don't always pop out the way they're supposed to. Mr. Gross was going to throw it out. Maybe you can fix it."

I was still mad, so I mumbled, "Thanks, Dad."

"How did you make out with the mechanical mouse? Did you get it fixed in time for that science project?"

Uh-oh—I had to be careful. I made it a rule never to lie to my dad. I just didn't always give him all the details. "It was a big success. Everyone loved it."

I guess he thought I wasn't saying much because he

11

had to go on that trip. "There's more to that surprise than silk flowers, Iggy," he said. "I was going to wait until I got back because I don't want you to think it's a bribe. But look into the bouquet."

I felt around and pulled out an envelope. "Let's just call it an early birthday present," he said.

My birthday wasn't until summer, but I wasn't going to argue—at least not until I checked the envelope. I opened it. Inside were four tickets to the Crusty Crew's summer rock concert in New York City. They were the most popular new group around, and their concerts were always sold out. "Dad, is this for real? Where did you get these?"

He laughed. "From Mr. Gross. He got them as part of a promotional package, but he can't stand rock music. So he asked me if I knew anyone who would like to go." He smiled at me. "You're too young to go to a rock concert by yourself, but if you don't mind me tagging along with you and your friends . . ."

"No, it'll be great. I can't wait."

"I have to hurry," he said. "Go say hi to Dottie. She's cooking dinner for you tonight—something home-cooked and healthy."

And then, as if on cue, Dottie Dumpler walked down the hall wearing headphones and whistling. "Iggy—I thought I heard your voice." She hadn't taken the headphones off, and her voice was loud enough for the neighbors to hear. "And you—Mr. Sands—you'd better get your handsome self moving," she added, brushing an invisible speck from his shoulder. "You don't want to be late."

Dad and I exchanged a look, and I thought we'd

12

both crack up. The Dumpster was always flirting with Dad.

Dad hurried into his trench coat and grabbed his suitcase. "Put those concert tickets away, Iggy. You don't want to lose them. They're as hard to get as snow in July."

As he left, the Dumpster put a meaty arm around my shoulder. "You're feeling a little bony, Iggy. I'll have to see if I can fatten you up a little. For dinner I am making galumpky—stuffed cabbage."

Yuck! I'd have to figure out a way to trash it.

"And for dessert," she added, winking at me, "a seven-layer chocolate cake with whipped cream topping."

Dottie was the world's best baker, and cake would make a much better dinner than lumpies. I just had to wait for a break.

At dinner the cabbage smelled, and the stuff inside—Dottie said it was meat and rice—was hard and dry. I poked around at it for a while, waiting to make my move, when the phone rang.

"I'll get it!" I yelled. "In my room." I grabbed my plate. "I'll eat while I'm talking." And before Dottie could argue, I was out the door. With my bedroom right down the hall, I got to the phone in two rings.

It was Drool, and as he talked to me, I opened my window and dumped the lumpy out.

"I had to call you, Iggy," he said. "Everybody was talking about you on the bus. All the guys were calling you a genius. And some of the girls, too."

"How did anyone know I had anything to do with it, Drool? You didn't tell anyone, did you?"

The silence that came out of the phone answered my question for me.

"I don't believe it! I swear. If you weren't my friend, I'd—"

"But wait, Iggy, wait till you hear this," Drool interrupted. "Here's the best part. A couple of the kids started saying maybe *you* should run for student council president."

I could feel my face get hot. "Don't be stupid. Candidates have to submit a petition of sixty names—*and* get a teacher recommendation. You know sixty kids who would sign a petition to make me president?"

"We could do it, Ig. You, Ed, and me."

I couldn't believe he was being serious. "How? By threats?" I tried to laugh, but somewhere inside me I wasn't laughing. My mind started to wander again, and I could see myself up onstage, thanking everybody for voting for me.

I don't know why, but that made me mad. "Forget it, Drool. I got about as much chance of getting nominated as I do of bringing Houdini back to life."

"Who?"

"Houdini—you never heard of Houdini? He was a famous magician who died a long time ago."

Drool's voice shivered as he asked, "You into witchcraft now? I don't want to have to deal with any ghosts."

He could be so dumb. "It was a joke. Look, forget about me for student council president. It's not going to happen. I've got to go. I'll see you tomorrow."

CHAPTER

3

The rest of that week was one of the weirdest of my life. Drool and Ed seemed to be busy all the time, huddling together and talking. Whenever I came near them, they would stop talking and start grinning.

"What's up?" I asked, the first time it happened.

"What do you mean?" Drool asked.

"I mean—what are you guys doing?"

Ed looked blank. "Doing? What do you mean—doing?"

"Forget it," I said, walking away. I expected them to come after me, but they didn't. They got right back into their huddle. I didn't bother asking again.

Later that week Ashley Douglas, who hardly ever talked to me, patted my arm and said, "I hope you feel better." She walked away before I could open my mouth to ask her what she was talking about.

By Friday I was so confused that I went home and left all my books in school. I was supposed to study for a big math test, but I didn't even know what chapter we were on. I thought of calling someone for help, but Murphy was mad at me, and Drool and Ed weren't any better at math than I was.

So when Mrs. Phister handed out the math test Monday morning, I had no idea where to start. It was all word problems, and they were the worst. I read the first one. *How long will it take a car, traveling 30 mph, to go 100 miles?* Who cared? Anyone who drove that slow didn't deserve to get where he was going anyway.

I chewed on my eraser. I tried to concentrate. My test paper was all messy where I had worked a problem, erased it, tried again, and erased again. A little hole was forming in the middle of the paper.

I dropped my pencil. As I bent down to pick it up, I tried to catch a quick look at the test on the desk next to mine. But that snobby Caitlen Cohane knew what I wanted. She looked at me like I was a clump of mud and then wrapped practically her whole body around her test paper, blocking my view.

I had to do something. I was getting desperate. I could pop a stink bomb. That would clear the room— *and* get me into big trouble.

Suddenly the P.A. system in the classroom crackled and clicked, and Dr. Harder's voice floated into the room. "Mrs. Phister, would you send Iggy Sands to the office, please?"

Everyone turned to look at me, and Mrs. Phister said, "He's in the middle of a test right now. Could he come in half an hour?"

"We have our assembly in half an hour. I'd like to see him now."

My neck felt all sweaty. Somebody must have squealed about the rat.

I stared at my test, wishing time would stop. I didn't answer when Mrs. Phister called my name. I hunched myself over my paper and pretended to be working.

Suddenly I saw her feet next to my desk. She put a hand on my shoulder. "Iggy, didn't you hear me? Or the announcement?"

I looked up at her, my face blank, like a turned-off television screen. "I'm sorry, what? I was working so hard, I guess I wasn't paying attention." I made sure my arms were covering my paper so she couldn't see the mess.

Caitlen said, "Oh, yeah, sure," and I wanted to smack her. I shot her a look, and she shut her mouth.

"Would you like to come back and finish up after school?" Mrs. Phister asked.

"I . . . ah . . . my father . . ." My mind was whirling. "He's calling me. From Buffalo. Right after school. I can't stay." It wasn't exactly a lie—he might call.

Mrs. Phister thought a minute. "Well, shall I grade you on what you've done?"

My mind was working overtime. "That wouldn't be fair. You always tell us to check so we don't make careless mistakes, and I didn't have time yet."

Mrs. Phister pulled in a deep breath and let it out. "I guess you'll have to take a makeup exam. You'd better get going. Dr. Harder seemed anxious to see you."

I rolled my math test into a tight ball, shoved it into my pocket, and left.

The sign on the secretary's desk in the main office said HAVE A NICE DAY. Some people have a lousy sense of humor. When she saw me, she smiled and said, "Go right in. Dr. Harder's expecting you, Iggy."

I flashed a big smile. "Do you know what she wants, Susan?" I had been there so much I figured we were on a first-name basis.

She just frowned and pointed to Dr. Harder's door.

Dr. Harder was sitting at her desk, studying some papers. A plush leather chair had been pushed in front of her desk, and when I came in, she motioned toward it and said, "Ah, Ignatius. Please. Sit down."

Hearing her say my real name sent a jolt of electricity through me. Why couldn't Dad have picked a regular name for me—like John or Nicholas. The chair she was pointing to looked like the electric chairs they used in old movies.

"That's okay. I can stand," I said. I tried to sound tough, but my voice came out a little high.

"Suit yourself, Ignatius. I thought you'd be more comfortable sitting." When I didn't move, she said, "Yes, well—I must say I'm rather surprised by this latest turn of events." She pointed toward some papers she was holding and said, "You've been busy. Very busy."

She was making me crazy. Why didn't she just say whatever she wanted to say?

I decided to tune her out. I started planning how I'd get even with all of them, everyone who was out to get me.

I was deciding to dump a load of worms into the teachers' lounge when I heard her say, ". . . had my doubts, but maybe you've turned over a new leaf." Then she stopped talking and started smiling.

What was going on? I must have looked confused because she stopped smiling. "You are serious about this, aren't you, Ignatius?" she asked. "When I got your petitions and this letter of recommendation, I assumed that meant you wanted to run for president. I've already talked to the other two candidates."

I couldn't seem to focus. I was having trouble breathing. "I think maybe I'll sit down," I said, easing myself into the chair.

She put her elbows on the desk, leaned close to me, and said, "Well, Ignatius? Was this your idea of a practical joke? A way to sabotage the school? Because if it is . . ." She left the words hanging like a threat.

I'm not sure exactly what happened then—or why. But I could feel power pouring into my body. I sat up taller. "I have no plans to sabotage anything. If I am elected president, I will do my best to . . . to . . . do my best."

She laughed. "You're starting to sound like a politician already. But getting yourself nominated is a long way from getting elected. I try very hard to keep this from being a popularity contest. Before the election in June, each candidate will have to plan and organize a class activity—that's to prove how much leadership and creativity you have. You will also have to help the other candidates with their activities—that's to show cooperation. *And* you must have a C-plus average to have your name placed on the ballot. Is that clear, Ignatius?"

She was still calling me *Ignatius*. But that was okay. It sounded kind of dignified, kind of . . . presidential.

Dr. Harder stood up. "The assembly will be starting

19

soon. You will sit on the stage with the other two candidates. When I introduce you, just stand. No speeches. I want the class to know who's running and explain the rules." She put her hand on the back of my neck. "I pride myself on running a disciplined school." She squeezed, just a little. "I'm sure you understand me."

Of course I did. She didn't trust me. She was even a little afraid of me—I could tell. Good. I didn't have a plan, not yet. But it wouldn't take much to think of one, and one thing I knew for sure—she'd be the last to know.

As I left her office, I felt like I had springs in my legs. I dug into my pocket, pulled out a piece of gum, and tossed it to Susan. "Have a nice day," I said as she smiled at me and started to unwrap it. I'd be long gone before her mouth started to burn from the pepper that was in it.

CHAPTER

4.

The lights onstage were hot, and I could feel a small river of sweat trickle down my back. I sat in between the other two kids who were running for president, waiting for the curtain to open.

On my right was Simon Ackmar, probably the smartest kid in the whole school, hunched over, reading a book. Simon got straight A's and played the flute in the school orchestra. He never smiled much, and I don't think he ever laughed.

But we were in this race together now, so I turned to him and held my hand out, palm up. "Hey, Simon, looks like we're running against each other. Slap me five, guy, and may the best man win."

Simon never even looked up.

I could feel my cheeks start to burn. I hated to be ignored. I leaned over close to him and, putting my finger on his shoulder, asked, "Hey, what's this? A bug?"

21

Simon's head jerked around to look, and as it did, I brought my fist up and caught him right under the chin. I didn't hurt him, but he was stunned. His head snapped back, and I could hear his teeth click together.

I gave him my phony smile. "I got him, Simon. The bug, I mean. It was crawling up under your chin. But I squashed it. Better wipe your chin, though. There might be some bug gunk left under it."

Simon glared at me and set his mouth in a straight line. "You're a savage, Sands," he said, barely moving his lips. "And believe me, there is one thing about this election that's certain. You won't even come in third." Then he went back to his book.

I took a deep breath. I reached into my jeans pocket and pulled out my plastic black widow spider that I kept close to me for special occasions. Holding it, I slapped Simon on the back. "No hard feelings, Simon."

"Get your hands off me, Sands," Simon said, shrugging.

"Right!" I said. I pulled my hand away and smiled. Velcro kept the ugly bug clinging to Simon's suit jacket.

I looked to my left. Dee Kruse, the Miss Popularity of Westford Elementary, was tapping her feet and jiggling her body. I looked for headphones, but she wasn't wearing any. I guess she was listening to music in her head.

I tried to think of something interesting to say to her. "Hey, Dee."

She stopped bouncing, stopped smiling, and looked over at me. She was making me feel small, so I sat up as high as I could. I had to say something really clever. "Failed any good tests lately?"

I knew she thought I was a jerk. I was waiting for her to say something nasty when she opened her mouth and let out a huge belch. Then the curtain opened.

I couldn't believe how strange it felt to be up there in front of the whole class. The auditorium lights were dimmed, but I could still see all the faces of the kids. A couple of them were whispering to each other and pointing. Others were laughing and giggling. Suddenly I felt like I was sitting there naked.

I didn't hear most of what Dr. Harder said. But when she said, "And now I will introduce this year's nominees for student council president," I tuned in.

I tried to look relaxed as she said, "I will introduce the candidates alphabetically by last name. Each of them will come to the podium and say a few words. I didn't tell them that they would be speaking, but I believe that a leader must be spontaneous, able to think on his or her feet."

I almost fell off my chair. She wanted me to get up there? To say something? I could feel my stomach get tight, my heart start to rattle. I'd have to think of something terrific. Serious? Funny? But what? What?

Dr. Harder continued, "Our first nominee is Simon Ackmar."

Simon slowly placed his book under his seat, walked to the podium, flattened his tie, and cleared his throat. "My fellow students," he began in a deep, rolling tone. "We, the students of Westford Elementary, are

23

great students, the best students to have passed through these halls of learning."

He paused. There was a general *"Huh? What's he saying?"* around the auditorium.

Simon waited a moment, like he was expecting a big burst of applause. When it didn't come, he put up his hand like he was silencing the crowd, and continued. "We need a president who will encourage that tradition of greatness. We need someone who is serious, intelligent, willing to work hard. I am that someone."

I couldn't believe it. How did Simon do it? How could a kid sound like he was forty? He even looked old.

He bowed slightly. A few kids clapped, some were hooting, but almost everyone was laughing.

When Simon turned to go back to his seat, the noise suddenly stopped. Kids started to whisper, then giggle, then laugh and point. Simon stopped, turned, and looked confused. The laughing got louder and I could hear Ed holler, "Call an exterminator! When's the last time you took a shower, Simon?"

Dr. Harder must have seen the bug on his back, too, because she hurried over to him, pulled it off, and held it in her fist. "It must have been a practical joke," she said quietly, walking with Simon back to his seat. She started to give me the famous stare, the one that's supposed to turn me into a rock. But I dropped my eyes to the floor and tried to look innocent.

Dr. Harder went back to the mike and said, "That's quite enough. One more outburst and you'll all be here after school." Silence came immediately.

"Our second candidate," Dr. Harder continued, "is Diedre Kruse."

Dee jumped up, plastered on a big smile, and bopped her way up to the podium. Holding her arms out like she wanted to hug the whole crowd, she said, "Hey, guys. You all know me." And, without warning, she started to rap.

> "Dee's my name, and fun's my game.
> I'm not a hick. I'm a cool-down chick.
> When the going gets tough, I'll never run,
> I'll find a way to make school fun.
> A vote for me is a vote for Dee,
> So come on, gang—let's all
> PAR-TEE!"

The kids went wild. Suddenly the last place I wanted to be was up there on that stage, ready to make a fool of myself. And then, as if the sound were coming through a long tunnel, I heard someone say, ". . . present to you our last nominee—Iggy Sands." I knew I had to get up and say something. But what?

I felt like I had weights hung all over my body. The auditorium was as quiet as a graveyard at midnight. When I got to the podium, I had to hold on to keep my knees from buckling. I looked into the waiting faces of my classmates, opened my mouth, and realized that I had absolutely nothing to say.

The seconds felt like hours. I knew I would faint. My eyes swept over the kids in the front row, and I wondered who would run up to catch me. I locked eyes with Caitlen Cohane. Miss Snobbo was sitting front row center, and she was staring at me. I hated her. I hated her long blond hair, her pretty face, her smart brain.

And then, without warning, she smiled at me. Not a nasty smile, but a warm, encouraging smile. And she winked. At the same time I heard Ed's voice start to chant: "Ig-gy, Ig-gy . . ." and then Caitlen joined in, "Ig-gy . . ." and before long it sounded like the whole auditorium was chanting my name and stomping their feet. My knees got strong, my hands stopped sweating, and the juice was pouring back into my brain.

I held up my hands, and the chanting stopped.

I didn't know what was going to come out, but I opened up my mouth and said, "I'm not one for a lot of talk—I believe in action. So—let's not think about it, let's just do it."

I had no idea what that meant. There was a split second of dead silence, and then they started to applaud—loud, echoing applause.

I loved it. I smiled and waved at them, like I had seen the President smile and wave on television just before he stepped into his private jet. And then I knew exactly what I wanted. I wanted to win that election.

CHAPTER

5

I didn't get a chance to talk to Drool and Ed until after school. When the last bell rang, we walked out together. No one said anything until we got to the playground.

Drool settled on the ground, legs crossed, and opened his book bag. Ed sat on a swing.

"So—tell me," I said. "I know you guys did it."

Drool reached into his bag and pulled out a Rinky Dink cupcake. "It all started as a joke," he finally said. "Ed and I wanted to see how many signatures we could get for you. Then, when it looked like we could get you nominated, we decided to go for it." He pulled the wrapper off the cupcake and took a small bite. He must have liked the taste, because he shoved the whole thing into his mouth. A little bit of white cream oozed down his chin.

I sat on a swing next to Ed. "But how did you get all those kids to sign?"

"It wasn't easy," he said, letting out a snort. I gave him a look, and he added quickly, "But it wasn't hard, either. You're pretty popular, you know."

I laughed. "Yeah, about as popular as a stink bomb. Come on. Tell me. How did you really do it?"

"Drool and I came up with a couple of stories. That's how we got most of them."

Drool reached for a bag of Cheese Bombs and tore it open. A couple spilled in his lap, and he scooped them up and shoved them into his mouth. "I went for sympathy. I told a couple of girls that you have some mysterious disease and might not even make it to elections. I told them that running for president was your last wish."

"And they believed you?" Then I remembered Ashley looking like she felt sorry for me. "What if they tell the teachers or Dr. Harder? We could get kicked out of school for spreading lies."

Drool stuffed his mouth again, chewed, and swallowed. "I'm not stupid. I told them I only found out by accident and that it's a big secret. That you'd probably die sooner if they told anyone."

"And isn't that the truth," I said. I turned to Ed. "How about you? How did you get kids to sign?"

A grin spread over his face. "The usual way. I concentrated on the boys, mostly. You know—a look, an elbow in the ribs, a word in someone's ear—worked every time. Besides, we only collected ten names to a sheet of paper. That way, no one knew how many signatures we really had. We let them think you'd never get enough. A lot of kids laughed when they signed."

I wasn't sure how that made me feel. "What about the teacher recommendation?" I asked.

Ed kicked the dirt, sending up a puff of dust. "That was easier than I thought it would be. I got it from Mr. Humphrey."

"Humphrey? He almost failed me in music. I thought he hated me."

"I thought so, too," Ed said. "That's why I decided to ask him—more of a challenge, you know. I started this long story about how you're really a good kid and how you really try and how you were too embarrassed to ask him yourself, but he cut me off. I was sure he'd say *forget it,* but he whipped out a piece of paper and wrote a recommendation right then."

"You're kidding!"

Ed grinned. "No, I'm not. He said he saw a lot of potential in you and he thought running for office would be a good experience, maybe help get you on the right path—you know, all that teacher stuff. Anyway, I took his recommendation, stuck it into an envelope with all the petitions, and put it in Dr. Harder's mailbox. The rest is history."

I didn't know what to say. "Thanks, guys. What do you think my chances are?"

Drool and Ed looked at me. "Chances for what?" Drool asked.

"Getting elected. What else?"

The two of them started laughing so hard I thought Drool would throw up the Cheese Bombs and Rinky Dinks he had eaten. Ed rolled off the swing, holding his sides.

"What's so funny?" I asked, standing up and looking down at them.

"You're a riot, you know that, Iggy?" Ed said, trying to catch his breath. "You know as well as we do what your chances of winning are—*ze-ro.* You'll get three votes: yours, Drool's, and mine."

I could feel my ears getting hot. "I knew that."

"We didn't do this to get you elected."

"I knew that," I said again. My cheeks were starting to burn.

Drool stood up, brushed dust and crumbs off his pants, and came over to me. Putting his arm around my shoulder, he said, "We knew you'd get a kick out of getting nominated. We wanted to see if we could do it without you finding out."

"Besides," Ed added, "we figured if we could get you nominated, we'd have it made for a while. We can cut classes and say we're campaigning."

"We can turn the school upside down," Drool said.

Ed was chuckling away, enjoying himself, when he suddenly got serious. He looked straight at me and asked, "You didn't really believe you could get elected, did you? I mean, you're not thinking of trying to get popular? Because you'd have to be stupid if—"

Enough was enough. I stomped over to him, stood over him, and said, "Don't call me stupid. Because I'm not. And don't tell me what to do. I know I don't have a shot at this election. But if we don't pretend we're serious, we won't get to put any of my plans into action because nobody's going to trust us. So don't *you* be stupid and blow this whole thing before it even gets started. You got me?"

"Hey, take it easy," Ed said, putting his arms up over his head as if I might take a shot at him. "Calm down. I didn't know you had any plans. What are they?"

I backed away. "Not now. I don't want to talk about them now." The truth was I had no plan. I didn't even have a plan for making a plan.

The next thing I knew, Simon had decided to get a head start on running his activity, a Saturday tag sale at the school. I couldn't believe I had agreed to help—to waste a whole Saturday morning on a stupid tag sale. But I had to show I was cooperative. All week I kept trying to figure out a way to get Ed and Drool to help.

Finally, at recess on Friday, I got around to telling them. Ed practically had a fit. "What do you mean, *we're going to help Simon with his tag sale?* Have you lost your mind?"

We were having a meeting in the corner of the playground. "I told you before," I said, not looking at them. "It's part of the plan. We have to look like we're serious about this campaign stuff. And all the candidates agreed to cooperate with each other."

Drool laughed. "Other candidates? You mean bean-brain Simon and Snooty Dee? Iggy, you're not getting serious about this election stuff, are you? We don't have to start handing out buttons and being nice to people, do we?"

I looked at Drool. He had a crust of ketchup on the corners of his mouth, and I wanted to tell him to go wash his face. Instead, I took a deep breath, looked right at him, and said, *"If* you want to help me with

31

the greatest practical joke this school has ever seen—*if* you want to be part of the greatest disaster in the whole world—one that will probably close school for at least two weeks if not more—and *if* you are truly my friend—you'll stop asking so many questions and do what I tell you to do."

Drool licked his mouth and the caked ketchup glistened. "Tell us what you got planned, Iggy."

"Yeah, Iggy. Tell us," Ed said. "Otherwise you can forget about us helping."

I knew I'd have to come up with something, but I didn't have the faintest idea what. Every time I tried to come up with one of my nasty or disgusting ideas, I'd see myself onstage, thanking the class for electing me president.

"It's a long-range plan," I said slowly. I could feel Ed and Drool staring at me. "The way I figure it, the way I see it"—suddenly, words started pouring out—"we bring in a lot of really ugly stuff. Awful stuff. Junk that no one would buy in a million years. Because if we don't cooperate, I get dumped from the campaign. And this way no one can say we didn't cooperate, and with any luck Simon's tag sale will be a big flop. Then we move on to stage two of Operation Sabotage."

Drool and Ed kept looking at me. Anyone with any sense would realize I didn't know what I was talking about. But sometimes Ed and Drool didn't have a whole lot of sense.

Ed started to nod, slowly at first, then faster. "Yeah. Okay. I can see where you're going with this. Yeah.

This is stage one. Help Simon but don't help him. Make sure his tag sale bombs."

"Right," I said. "So find some awful junk for the tag sale tomorrow."

"That might be a problem," Drool said, wiping his mouth with his arm. A wad of spit hung on his sleeve.

I clenched my teeth. Drool had always done what I told him to do. No questions asked. "What do you mean, 'It's a problem'? Maybe *you're* the problem. Maybe I don't need a slob like you for a friend. Who needs a friend with a gob of spit on his arm anyway?"

Drool pulled back. He looked at me, looked at his sleeve, and, wiping it on the back of his pants, said, "I just meant that we don't have any junk at home. My mom's a neat freak. You've been to my house. She's in a war with clutter."

My cheeks started to burn. I put my arm around Drool's shoulder. "I forgot about your mother. Listen, come home with me. We've got so much stuff around, we could clean out half the attic, and my dad wouldn't care. He keeps saying we've got to get rid of all the junk up there." I looked at Ed. "Want to come?"

"Why not," Ed answered. "Maybe I can find something, too."

CHAPTER

6

When we walked through my front door, there was the Dumpster, standing in front of us. "I brought some friends home, Dottie. I hope that's okay," I said.

She looked Ed and Drool up and down. "It all depends," she said.

"On what?" I asked. I couldn't figure out why the Dumpster was giving us a hard time.

"On how hungry you are," she answered and broke into a big smile. "I just baked peanut butter cookies. They're in the kitchen."

Drool took off like a shot. I could smell the warm sweet smell of cookies. "Thanks, Dottie," I said as Ed and I headed for the kitchen.

Drool's jacket was in a heap on the floor. He was sitting at the counter munching on a cookie. "These are the best," he said.

I poured three glasses of milk.

"I can't figure out why you and your dad live

alone in such a big house," Ed said, reaching for a cookie.

"I don't know," I said. "I think my father bought it when he married my mother. Then later, it was too much trouble to move."

Drool dunked a cookie in his milk. Without looking at me he asked, "You ever hear from her?"

"Who?"

"Your mother," Drool said. "I mean, don't you ever wonder about her?"

Ed coughed and poked Drool so hard he practically fell off the stool.

Drool jumped up and shoved Ed. "Hey, what did you do that for?"

"Because you're stupid," Ed said, shoving him back.

They were starting to get real loud, so I went over, pulled them apart, and stood between them. "Knock it off. For your information, no, I don't wonder about my mother. I have my dad, and that's all I need. Come on, are we going to look for stuff for the tag sale or not? Put your glasses in the sink and follow me—there's a back staircase we can use. That way, the Dumpster won't ask a lot of questions."

I hadn't been up to the attic in a long time, and when I opened the door, Drool wrinkled his nose and said, "Pee-uuu. What's that smell?"

I started backward up the narrow staircase and whispered, "Everything's been closed up. Just be quiet and follow me."

"It smells like the inside of a grave," Drool whispered back.

35

I stopped. "How do you know what a grave smells like?"

Drool shrugged. Ed, coming up behind us, asked, "Why are we whispering?"

Drool just shrugged again.

When I got to the top, I felt a cold shiver run down my legs. I pulled a string, and a bare light bulb went on. The whole place smelled like warm mothballs.

"Do you believe in ghosts?" Drool whispered.

"Why?" Ed whispered back. "Do you?"

"Not usually. But if I did, this would be a perfect spot for them to hide."

"Don't be such a wimp," I said and gave Drool a shove. But my voice sounded too loud, so I added in a whisper, "There's no such thing as ghosts."

Ed was bending down, squinting at the floor. "There's dust on the floor."

"So what?" I was getting impatient. "It's not like Drool's mother comes up here and cleans, you know."

"Yeah, I know," Ed said quietly. "But there's footprints in the dust. See them?"

Drool bent down next to Ed. "I sure do. Let's get out of here."

I was about to say okay when I thought about the election again. No ghosts or scared friends were going to stop me now. I sucked in my breath. "They must be mine. I come up here sometimes."

I started to take a step across the floor. It groaned. I stopped and turned. "You going to stand there like a couple of statues?"

"You sure it's safe?" Drool asked.

"Sure," I said. "I've been up here lots of times." It

wasn't exactly true. I hardly ever came up here because the place gave me the creeps. But I couldn't tell them that.

The three of us walked slowly in a tight bunch.

"I have to go home soon," Ed said. "Let's just find some stuff, shove it in an empty box, and get out of here."

We started looking around. Ed found a statue of a woman with a clock in her belly and one foot broken off, and I added a lopsided basket filled with faded plastic fruit. As Drool tossed a doll onto the pile—her face lined with cracks and her orange hair a matted tangle—he asked, "Not yours, is it, Iggy?"

I answered him by throwing a green cushion at him that had SOUVENIR OF NIAGARA FALLS embroidered on it in purple. It hit Drool with a soft thump and sent a cloud of dust up around his head.

We had stopped worrying about ghosts. It was like a big scavenger hunt, a contest to see who could find the ugliest of the uglies.

I went by myself toward the farthest corner of the attic and, behind a chimney stack, found a large black trunk under a high, dirty window. The lid creaked a little as I opened it, and the musty smell of old clothes drifted out.

Something told me to close the trunk and walk away. Instead, I reached in and pulled out an old leather scrapbook. It had been resting on a pile of clothes—a black tuxedo, a white dress that sparkled with sequins, and even a shiny top hat.

On the scrapbook cover were the words MONDO THE MAGNIFICENT engraved in gold. Inside, each page was filled with pictures and newspaper clippings that dated back to before I was born. All the articles were about a young magician who traveled around the country with his beautiful assistant and amazed audiences with death-defying tricks. The headlines said things like, *"Mondo the Magnificent Escapes Death Once Again,"* and *"Is Mondo the reincarnation of Houdini?"* There were a lot of pictures of my father. He was younger and he was dressed all in black except for the red lining of his cape—but I recognized him.

I couldn't believe it. I knew my father had been a magician, but I always thought he did amateur stuff like kids' birthday parties. I never thought about him being a *real* magician. And it didn't take a genius to figure out that his assistant was my mother.

At the back of the album was a letter—very short, very fancy handwriting. "Dear Armondo—the world needs me. I know you understand. Take care of our son. Affectionately, Anna."

I heard footsteps behind me. Shoving the letter back into the album and shutting it, I whirled around. Ed stood there.

"What did you find?" he asked. "Any more uglies?" He started to smile, then stopped. "What's the matter?"

"Nothing," I said. "There's nothing good here." I didn't want Ed to see the scrapbook or the letter and start asking a lot of questions.

I turned back to the trunk and, pushing back the fancy clothes, plunged the scrapbook down under them as far as I could. But I scratched my hand on something sharp and yelped with the pain.

"Iggy? What is it? Are you okay?" Ed put his hand on my shoulder, but I shrugged it off. My hands were still in the trunk.

I didn't know why, but I felt dizzy. I rummaged around for whatever had scratched me, felt a cold, boxlike thing, and pulled it out, untangling it from silk scarves and fancy clothes. The attic was hot and stuffy, but I could feel a cold sweat trickle down my face.

Turning slowly back to Ed, I held a tarnished silver box covered in bumpy designs, like snakes twined all around it. Their eyes were small red stones that winked in the fading light of the window, but some of the stones had fallen off, and there were spots of flaking glue. One corner was jagged, and that's what must have cut my hand.

"Wow! What's that?" Ed asked in a hoarse whisper. He reached out to touch the box but pulled his hand away quickly, as if it were hot.

"I don't know," I said.

We stood there, staring at the box. I felt like we would be there forever, trapped in some weird time warp.

Suddenly Drool hollered, "Hey, guys, where'd you go?" And the spell was broken.

Drool came over and saw the box. "That's it. You win the prize. That's the most ugly thing in this whole attic."

"I'm putting it back," I said.

Drool frowned. "Why? I thought you wanted to bring the worst-looking stuff to Simon's tag sale. You can't get much worse than that. Bring it over to the steps where we can get a good look at it." He saw

39

the open trunk behind me. "Anything else in there?" he asked, taking a step forward and reaching out a hand.

"Nothing," I said quickly, cradling the box under my left arm and slamming the trunk shut.

"Hey," Drool yelped. "Watch it! You almost took my arm off."

I ignored him and, holding the box, led the way back toward the steps. "Come on. Let's get this junk downstairs. I want to see what's in this box."

CHAPTER

7

We stashed the junk in my closet. Then we examined the box, looking for a lid, a way to open it, but we couldn't find one. We turned it over and over. I tapped it against the floor, careful not to knock any more of the red stones off it.

"Maybe it's solid," Ed said.

"I don't think so," I answered, shaking it. "It sounds like there might be something in it."

"Sounds empty to me," Ed said. "Stop wasting your time. Stick it in the tag sale with the other stuff. Who knows, maybe somebody will buy it. I mean, if anybody goes to the sale. Simon didn't do much advertising. I still don't see much point in going."

I decided it was time for a bribe. "If you help out tomorrow, I'll treat you to the Burger Factory afterward—anything you want." I knew Drool would like that.

I was right. "You've got a deal, Iggy old pal. I'm sure my mom will give us a ride in the morning."

41

I looked at Ed. "What do you say, Ed? Are you with us?"

He shrugged his shoulders and said, "Why not? I've always wanted to waste Saturday going to school. We'll see you tomorrow."

After they left, I made sure I had enough money to treat them to lunch. I was saving for a video game, but I never broke promises to friends.

The next morning, after we unloaded our box of junk at school, Ed said, "I hope we don't have to hang around too long. I've got better things to do." I knew Ed was feeling grouchy again. He thought it was crazy to come to school on a Saturday.

The tag sale was set up on the ball field at the back of the school. Dr. Harder and a lot of the teachers were helping, but it was pretty pathetic-looking—about a dozen tables set up with a little bit of stuff on each one. I could see Simon, dressed in crisp new jeans and a starched shirt, running around being the big boss. He spotted us and came hustling over.

"You're late, Sands," he said.

I looked at my watch. "It's only nine-fifteen, Simon."

He was looking through the stuff in our box, making a face. "And I told you to be here at nine, Sands. The sale is over at one."

Ed was about ready to pick Simon up and use him for a football. I stepped between them. "I'm here, Simon. I said I'd help and I will. Where do you want us to go?"

"Take the table at the end over there—next to Caitlen and Dee," he said and scuttled off.

Caitlen—I don't know why, but her name made me

smile. Then Ed snapped, "Oh, terrific. Just what we need. An afternoon with the snob and the belcher."

As we walked toward our table, I saw Murphy with two of his friends. I stopped at his table and said, "How's it going?" I was hoping he'd forgotten about our argument. I never knew when I might need his help.

He looked up. "You here to apologize, Iggy?"

I could feel my cheeks getting hot. Ed and Drool were watching. "Like I told you," I said. "There's nothing I'm sorry for."

"Then just keep walking," he said and went back to arranging some stuff on the table.

"What was that about?" Drool asked.

"Nothing," I said. "Murphy's just being thick-headed, that's all. But he'll come around."

We put the clock, the basket of fruit, and the other stuff on the table. I put the silver box in the middle. I had to laugh at how ugly it really was—tarnished silver with chips of dull red glass. I thought of what Mrs. Phister told us once—great minds have great imaginations. That was me—a great mind.

Dee walked over and stood in front of us with her hands on her hips. "I didn't know cockroaches got up so early," she said, picking up the box.

"Who you calling a cockroach?" Drool asked.

"Ignore her," I said. "Frogs aren't worth talking to." I reached over, took the box out of her hand, and set it back on the table. "Don't touch if you don't want to buy."

She wrinkled her nose. "Buy that thing?" She wiped

her hands on her pants. "I just hope it doesn't give me warts."

As she turned to walk away, I put my thumbs in my ears and stuck out my tongue. She made me want to scream.

Drool, Ed, and I sat behind the table. A couple of people wandered over and looked at our stuff, but nobody bought anything. At least no one could say I didn't help.

After a while Ed started to get squirmy. "I don't see how this is such a great plan. Did you bring some stink bombs? Or shaving cream? Or toilet paper? *Anything* fun?"

When I didn't answer, he stood up and said, "Come on, Drool. Iggy can stay here and grow roots. Let's look for some action." He turned to me. "We'll see you later," he said. "For lunch."

I settled in my chair, pulled my baseball hat over my eyes, and decided to snooze awhile.

I heard a frilly little laugh from the table next to me, and without moving my head, I shifted my eyes in that direction. Caitlen was talking to Dee. She threw her head back when she laughed, and her blond hair bounced and shimmered in the sunlight. I knew she was Dee's best friend, but she wasn't as snotty as Dee—at least not lately. I could see her glancing in my direction once in a while, but I pretended not to notice. She was probably impressed by how casual I was.

Suddenly she turned and walked over to my table. She pushed back my baseball hat and smiled, the same smile she had given me when I was onstage. "Hi, Iggy," she said. "How's it going?"

44

My mind raced. I was trying to think of something dazzling to say. "It's going good." I sounded like I had marbles in my mouth.

She started to look through the stuff on the table, and all of a sudden I felt embarrassed. I knew she would make fun of the junk that was there.

"Where did you get all this?" she asked.

"My attic," I said. "Just some odds and ends that have been up there for a long time."

"It's really neat stuff. I think I'll buy something from you."

She was being so nice I thought I would melt.

Just then Dr. Harder walked over. "The tag sale's almost over," she said. "I'm collecting any money you have from sales so that I can make a deposit." She looked at my table. "It doesn't look as if you've sold much."

It was hard to concentrate on Dr. Harder with Caitlen so close. "I—ah—we—"

Caitlen picked up the lady with the clock in her stomach. "I'm going to buy something, Dr. Harder," she said. She put down the clock and picked up the silver box. I felt a knot in my stomach. *Not the box,* I thought.

"I'll take this," Caitlen said. "How much is it?"

"You don't want that," I said, taking it from her and putting it back down. "How about the basket of fruit? It's only fifty cents."

"I don't want the fruit. I want the box," she said and picked it up again.

All of a sudden I didn't want to sell the box, not

without knowing if something was in it. "It's not for sale," I said, taking it from her again.

Dr. Harder was watching me. "I'm not sure I understand," she said. "Why don't you want to sell the box? You did bring it to sell, didn't you?"

"It's sold," I blurted out. "I forgot. Someone came before and paid for it. That's why I can't sell it."

Dr. Harder raised her eyebrows. "Why didn't you say so?" She held out her hand and I realized she wanted money. When I didn't move right away, she squinted at me and asked, "You *are* planning to donate that money to the class, aren't you? You didn't come here to make money for yourself, did you?"

I started to sweat. "No. Of course not. I mean—" I reached in my pocket and pulled out the money I had taken with me.

Dr. Harder took it and said, "Someone paid quite a bit of money for the box, Iggy. Why did they leave it here?"

I was having trouble thinking because Caitlen was standing there, watching me.

I stood up and started rearranging the stuff on the table. "My neighbor bought it. I told her I'd deliver it. I just forgot for a minute. You don't want me to sell it twice, do you?"

That seemed to satisfy Dr. Harder. "Of course not. No one was accusing you of anything. It's just that Dee told me she didn't think you had sold anything."

I was about to say something really nasty when Caitlen said, "Well, I guess she was wrong. Dee sometimes jumps to conclusions."

I looked at her. Why was she being so nice? Maybe

46

she was starting to realize what a super guy I was. I took off my hat, smoothed back my hair, and flashed her a smile, but she was looking at Dr. Harder.

"Be sure to clean up before you leave," Dr. Harder said. She walked away, and suddenly I realized that Caitlen was about to go, too.

"Ah . . . Caitlen?" I called.

She turned. What was she thinking? I wished I could read minds. And then she smiled, and it was like a rainbow was glowing all around her.

"I'm sorry about the box," I said. "Look—pick out something else. Anything. No charge."

"That's okay, Iggy. If you—if your neighbor changes her mind about the box, let me know. I'd like to find out what's in it." And she turned and left.

I looked at the box in my hand. Another piece of red glass had fallen off, and a flake of dried yellow glue fluttered into my hand. What a dope. All I had to do was give Caitlen the box, and she'd probably fall in love with me for life. And what did I do instead? Lied to Caitlen and donated to Simon's tag sale the money I was going to use to treat the guys.

CHAPTER

8

While we waited for Drool's mother to pick us up, Drool said, "Okay, here's the plan. We'll stop at your house, Iggy, and drop off this stuff. Then Mom will drop us at the Burger Factory so we can chow down, then—"

"Forget it," I said, cutting him off. "We can't go."

"What do you mean, *We can't go?* You said if we helped, you'd treat. Well, we helped—now you treat."

I could feel my ears getting hot. "I don't have any money."

Ed was just standing there, watching and listening. His face started to look like a storm brewing. Finally he asked, "What's going on, Iggy?"

"Nothing's going on," I said. "I had the money. And I was going to treat. But Dr. Harder took it."

"So go get it back," Drool whined. "I'm hungry."

Ed waited until Drool finished, never taking his eyes off me. "She took it? Or you gave it to her?" When

I didn't answer he said, "I thought so. We didn't sell anything, so you donated money to Simon's tag sale. Unbelievable!"

"It wasn't like that," I said. I wanted to explain, but I knew they wouldn't understand.

Just then Drool's mother pulled up. All the way to my house no one said a word—except Drool's mother, who kept asking how we made out and if we had a good time and what we did. When no one answered her, even she stopped talking.

When we got to my house, I said, "You could have lunch here."

But Ed mumbled something about having to get home, and Drool just kept sulking.

Dottie must have been out shopping because no one was around. I dragged the stuff into the house and put it back in my closet, except for the box that had caused all the trouble. I put that outside in the garbage.

Five minutes later I picked it out, looked at it, and threw it away again. But something kept bothering me, like a pebble in my shoe. So I fished it out, brought it in my room, and put it on my dresser. I decided to find a screwdriver or a hammer to force the thing open.

I put my finger on one of the snake eyes that looked ready to fall off, and suddenly the box snapped open. Just like that—I had barely touched it. There must have been a hidden spring that got triggered off somehow. But it gave me the chills.

Inside was nothing but a small book with a black leather cover, but the title was too faded to read. I brought it over to the window and opened it. On the first page someone had handwritten in fancy letters, "Conjure Magic." I had no idea what that was.

The book had only six pages, the paper so old and yellow that I thought it would crumble in my hands. On the top of the first page it said *Prologue*. As I started to read, I could feel my scalp getting all prickly.

> In a graveyard small and simple
> Three great minds as one shall be.
> After solemn incantation
> Face the depths of mystery.
> Midnight, moonlight, myth, and madness
> Raise the spirits of the dead.
> Phantom figure cold will follow
> When the words have all been said.

I wasn't exactly sure what it all meant, but I did know that this was a book about how to make a ghost appear. My hands started to get cold, like they were holding a big chunk of ice. I imagined a grave opening up somewhere.

I should have stopped reading. I should have shoved the book back in the box and gotten rid of it. I didn't want to get myself mixed up with any ghosts. Uh-uh, not me. I had enough problems.

But I couldn't stop. The writing was hard to read, but the directions seemed pretty easy. Get a whole bunch of weird stuff. Then, with two other people at midnight, draw some signs in the dirt and say a few words. Charts were included.

It didn't say what would happen after that, but my imagination had a pretty good idea.

When I called Drool and Ed and told them what I had found in the box, they were at my door within ten minutes. The two of them sat down and studied the book harder and longer than I'd ever seen them with a book before in my life.

Ed finally looked up and said, "Let's try it."

"Are you nuts?" Drool asked. I was glad he said it because that was exactly what I was thinking.

"Come on," Ed said. "Don't be such a chicken. What have we got to lose?"

Our lives, I wanted to say. But of course I didn't.

"Okay," Ed said. "Then that's settled. Let's see what we have to get and when we're going to try this."

I had to show I wasn't scared, so I took the book. "Drool, get a piece of paper and a pencil from the desk over there," I said. "We'll make a list of what we need and figure out who's going to get what."

Drool rummaged through the mess on the desk and finally came up with a sheet of paper and a stubby, chewed-on pencil.

"I'll read through this slowly," I said. "You write down what we need.

> Salt and ashes tied in silk
> Tombstone moss and sour milk
> Two cat's whiskers tipped with mud
> Chicken bones and fresh bat's blood
> Three sharp daggers, silver bright
> Three tall candles, black as night.
> Voices join in ancient song
> Spirits dancing all night long.

"Okay. That's it. You got it all?"

Drool was still writing, but he said, "Yeah, I got it. Now what?"

"That's easy," I said. "Now we decide who's getting what."

It was quiet for a minute. I knew what we were all thinking—who was going to get tombstone moss? And how were we going to get bat's blood?

"Let's write them down and draw out of a hat," Ed suggested. "There are ten things, but we can put salt and ashes together. Then we each pick three."

We did, and on my first draw I got the daggers. On the second I got silk. I held my breath as I pulled the third paper. I'd been pretty lucky so far. I slowly unfolded the paper and read *bat's blood*. I felt weak.

Drool was complaining about tombstone moss, so I asked, "Want to trade?" and I showed him my last pick.

"Are you nuts?" He frowned. "Where you gonna get bat's blood?"

"From a bat, stupid. Where do you think?" And I smiled as they looked at me with awe.

"When are we doing this?" Ed asked.

"Tonight," I said. "Midnight. Meet me right outside my window."

CHAPTER

9

They tapped on my window at eleven-thirty. I had stuffed some pillows under my blankets in case Dottie checked on me. She'd think I was asleep.

I opened my window, and Ed stuck his head in. "You got everything? Don't forget the book. We need the directions."

"It's all here," I answered, handing him a bag. "Be careful you don't cut yourself on the daggers."

I grabbed a flashlight and climbed out of the window. "Let's check that we have everything. Ed, what did you bring?"

"I've got salt and ashes in this plastic container, a couple of chicken legs left over from dinner, and three candles," he said, holding each item out for us to see.

"The candles are supposed to be black," I said. "Not red."

"We didn't have any black ones. These were left

over from Christmas. Besides, at night you can hardly tell the difference."

"And you were supposed to bring bones, without the meat."

"We'll have to eat it first," Drool said and reached for a chicken leg.

Why argue. "How about you, Drool? I have you down for tombstone moss, two cat's whiskers, and sour milk."

He tossed the chicken bone back to Ed. "Here's the moss," he said, pulling a hunk of green stuff from his bag.

"You got it from a tombstone?" I asked.

"It's moss. And here's the milk," he added quickly, holding up a jar. It was sour milk, all right—all curdled and lumpy and disgusting-looking.

"Wow," I said. "I never thought you'd find sour milk at your house."

"I didn't," he said. "I got some fresh milk and poured vinegar in it. Instant sour milk. But don't open the jar—it smells like bad breath. And I got the cat's whiskers," he said. But he didn't pull them out.

I was suspicious. "Let me see," I said.

"Why?" he asked. "Don't you trust me?"

"Just let me see them."

As he dug into his bag he said, "I almost got into big trouble because of these. I was holding our cat and was just about to pull out two whiskers when my mother came into the room and saw me. She started screaming at me. She scared me and the cat so much that the cat took off, and I couldn't find her all afternoon." He finally found what he had been searching for and handed them to me.

I shined the flashlight on them, but they were hard to see. "They feel like plastic," I said.

"They are," Drool said.

"You were supposed to get cat's whiskers," Ed said.

"They *are* cat's whiskers," Drool said. "When my mother scared the cat away and I was looking for her, I found a toy stuffed cat that my father won at the carnival. I got the whiskers there."

"From a *stuffed cat?*"

Drool snatched the whiskers back from me and put them in his bag. "The directions didn't say they had to be from a *real* cat, did they? It just said *cat*. These are from a cat. And if they're not good enough, I'll go home. I'm starting to think this is all stupid, anyway."

I didn't want him to leave. "The whiskers are fine. Come on, we'd better get going."

"Not so fast," Ed said. "Let's see your stuff."

"Oh, right. It's all here. Silk," I said, pulling out a piece of red material that I had cut from one of the old tricks my father had brought home. "Three daggers . . ."

"They're not daggers," Drool said. "They're kitchen knives."

"That's all we had. At least they're not plastic," I said. That shut Drool up. "And . . ." I pulled out a small jar that I held concealed in my hand. Leaning close to them, I whispered, "Bat's blood."

Drool took a step back. "No kidding. Where'd you get it?"

"I went back up to the attic," I said, making my

voice slow and dramatic. "And there they were—bats—in a dark corner. And before they knew what hit them, I had sliced one of them open and let his blood drip into this jar."

Drool stood there, looking paralyzed. Ed reached for the jar, and before I could stop him, he took it and unscrewed the top. He brought it close to his face, trying to look into it. Suddenly he started sniffing. Then he looked at me and frowned. "It smells like ketchup," he said.

I snatched the jar back, screwed the cover on, and stared at him. "You ever smell bat's blood before?" I asked.

He thought for a minute before answering. "No. I guess not."

"Well," I said, putting the jar into my bag. "It just so happens that bat's blood and ketchup smell a lot alike. I was as surprised as you when I cut that bat open and smelled that blood. If you don't believe me, let's go back up to my attic. You can find another bat and get the blood, if you want to."

"No, that's okay," Ed said quickly. "Besides, it's almost midnight. Where are we going to do this chanting stuff?"

"The book said we have to do it in a graveyard," Drool said. His voice cracked.

"Don't worry. I know just the place," I said and led the two of them through a wooded area at the back of my house. I stopped when we came to a small clearing.

"This is a graveyard?" Ed asked.

"Kind of," I said. "See those little wooden crosses? This is where I buried my turtle, two goldfish, and a

56

snake I found on the road when it was squashed by a car."

Drool and Ed looked relieved. I guess they didn't want to go into a people-type graveyard any more than I did. Besides, being in the woods at night, even with the moon out, was spooky enough. The wind moaned through the high branches of the trees, and a dog or something howled in the distance.

"Let's get this over with," Ed said. "This whole thing is making me feel weird."

"Yeah, me, too," Drool said. "Maybe we should forget about it."

"Come on," I said. "It won't take long."

"But what happens if it works?" Drool asked. "What are we going to do if we really do make a ghost appear?"

"We'll worry about that later," I said.

Using the daggers, we drew a large circle in the dirt and a star with six points inside of that. We added some scribbles and squiggly lines, like it showed in the book. Then we put the bones in the middle, and on top of them we put the cat's whiskers, the salt and ashes tied up in the silk, and the tombstone moss. We sprinkled it all with the sour milk and the bat's blood. The stink made me hold my breath.

"Now for the candles," I said. "We light them, hold one in our right hand and a dagger in our left. Then we stand inside the circle and read the chant together." As I handed Ed and Drool a candle, I said, "Give me the matches, Ed."

He looked at me. "What matches? You didn't say anything about bringing matches."

"How did you think we were going to light the candles? Rub two sticks together?"

"Matches weren't on my list."

I took a deep breath and counted to ten. It didn't matter anyway. What ghost with any sense at all would bother with us?

"So we won't light the candles," I said. "Just hold them while we read the chant. I printed it on this piece of paper." I had a problem figuring how to hold the candle, the dagger, the flashlight, and the piece of paper, but I solved it by spearing the paper with the dagger and holding the flashlight and the candle together.

Drool and Ed huddled in close, and I said, "Okay—on the count of three we'll start. One—two—"

"Wait a minute," Drool said. "What language is that? The words don't make any sense."

"That's why I printed them out. They're not hard. Just read."

We stumbled through the first four lines of the chant:

> *"ZEG NA RU FA*
> *MOR TA VAM*
> *JEN DA LOO NA*
> *VER GIN NAM"*

When we got to the last line, Ed and Drool started to laugh. I was the only one chanting *SHIN GARD, SHIN GARD, SHIN GARD.*

"Come on, you guys, get serious!" I yelled.

Ed, between snorts, asked, "Shin gard? What—is this ghost a soccer player?" Then he and Drool started dancing around, slapping each other's hands, and Ed was chanting, "Shin gard, soccer ball, goal, shoot, score!"

And Drool, laughing, chanted, "I'm going on home—I can't take no more."

"You're a poet," Ed said. Laughing and slapping each other on the back, they started to walk away.

"Don't go yet," I called. "Wait just a little longer."

"For what?" Ed asked. "No ghost is going to show up. This was a stupid idea. Besides," he said, looking right at me, "I thought you didn't believe in ghosts."

"I don't," I said. "It was your idea to try this."

"No, it wasn't," he said. "It was Drool's idea."

"No, it wasn't," Drool said. "I just came along for the laughs. But now I'm cold and tired. I'm going home."

As Ed and Drool started to walk away, Ed turned and asked, "Aren't you coming, Iggy?"

"Later. We did all this stuff. I want to hang around just for a little while. See if anything happens." I wanted something to happen. With the election, and Caitlen, and all the other stuff going on, I could use a little help from a ghost.

"Nothing's going to happen," Ed said. "Except that my father might kill me if he catches me sneaking into the house after midnight."

"You could stay in my room," I said. But either they didn't hear me or they didn't want to. And there I was—all by myself with a circle and a star and a bunch of smelly stuff.

CHAPTER

10

I sat by myself on a log for a long time—listening.

I thought I heard a branch crack under someone's foot. I thought I heard a sigh. I thought I heard a ghost howl. I wanted something to appear and make my life easy. But it was all my imagination. I tried to remind myself that great minds have great imaginations, but it didn't do any good. I was feeling stupid—and cold.

I got the three kitchen knives and the book and trudged home. I climbed through my window, closed it, and turned around.

My heart jumped. There—in my bed—someone was sleeping. With my pulse racing and my legs feeling like rubber bands, I crept closer, reached out, and pulled off the covers. But it was only the pillows I had stuffed under my blanket.

I turned on my light, sat on the bed, and looked at the book that was supposed to call up a ghost. What a joke.

I opened the book and read through the chant again. When I got to the last line, the soccer-player line, my stomach did a flip. It didn't say *shin gard*—I must have copied it wrong. It said *shun gad*. But so what? It wouldn't have worked anyway.

I dropped the book on the floor, put my head in my hands, and mumbled, *"Shun gad, shun gad, shun gad."* Suddenly I felt a blast of ice cold air, and the bed moved as someone sat down next to me.

I turned my head slowly. I saw a boy about my age, but he was wearing a tall black fur hat, a heavy coat, and leather boots up to his knees. Snow covered his hat and shoulders.

We were face to face, no more than two inches apart, staring at each other. Neither one of us moved for a few seconds. It was like time had stopped.

And then, barely moving his lips, he whispered, "What are you looking at?"

I stood up and took a step backward. His question was so silly that I forgot to be afraid. "You. I'm looking at you. Where'd *you* come from?"

He stood up, took off his hat, and shook it. Water drops spattered all over. He put the hat carefully on the bed and turned to me. "You called me here, didn't you? The book, the woods, all that chanting with your friends. Not that you did it right, of course. *'Shin gard'?* That was pretty stupid."

As I stood in front of him, listening to him insult me, I had the strange feeling I was looking in a mirror. "You know what? Except for those clothes, you look just like me," I said.

He came a little closer and looked me up and down. "Well, for heaven's sake. I hope not."

"What's that supposed to mean?"

He stepped back. "Don't be so touchy. I just don't think I look anything like you."

"Yes, you do. Come over here. I'll show you." I walked to the mirror and he followed. We were standing side by side, but I was the only one in the mirror.

"You're not there," I said.

"Yes, I am," he said. "I can see both of us. And believe me, we don't look anything alike."

A million questions were boiling around in my head. "So where did you come from?" I asked. "And how did you get here? And what's your name? And *why* are you here?"

"Not so many questions," he said. "You can call me Nicholas. But I don't know. Why *am* I here?"

Just my luck—a dumb ghost. I reached out to touch him, but he backed away. "Are you real?" I asked.

"Do I look real?"

"Yes, but—"

"Then I'm real. Now—what do you want?"

I couldn't believe my luck. This was the chance of a lifetime. "I'd like a million dollars," I said.

He laughed. "You're kidding. What do I look like, some cheap genie who popped out of a lamp?"

Terrific. Not only was he dumb, he thought he was a comedian, too. "You asked me what I wanted. What can you do for me?"

"It all depends."

"On what?"

"On how much you can do for yourself. Actually, I'm pretty good at giving advice."

"Advice? That's it? I go through all that trouble to get you here, and all you can do is talk?" I balled up my fists, ready to take a swing at him. "I don't need talk—I need action."

Without saying a word, Nicholas reached up in the air, grabbed at something, and threw it at me. A snowball hit me right in the head. "Hey!" I hollered, as another one hit me in the arm. "Cut it out." I ducked as two more whizzed by and hit the wall.

He snatched another one out of the air, patted it, and said, "I thought you wanted action."

Suddenly I heard Dottie Dumpler right outside my door saying, "Iggy? What's going on? Are you all right?" I turned toward the door just as she started to open it.

My mind was racing, but I couldn't think straight. I wondered what she'd say when she saw someone else in my room at two o'clock in the morning chucking snowballs around. Especially someone who looked like me in funny clothes.

She stood in the door, a fuzzy pink bathrobe pulled tight around her heavy body.

"I—ah—I can explain. This is—I want you to meet—" and I turned to introduce the Dumpster to Nicholas.

But he wasn't there. I stood with my mouth open, looking at nothing.

She came over to me. "Meet who? What are you talking about?" She walked toward the place where he had been standing, stopped suddenly, and shivered.

Turning up the collar on her robe, she asked, "Why is it so cold in here?" Then, reaching down and picking up a small hunk of snow, she frowned. "Is this snow?"

"Snow? You think that's snow?" My voice wasn't working quite right, but my brain was doing okay. "That's not snow. It just looks like snow. I had some ice water. With crushed ice. I must have dropped some."

She looked closer at her hand, but there was nothing but a small puddle of water. "It looked like snow," she said, shaking her head.

I tried to change the subject. "How come you're up so late?"

"I couldn't sleep, so I went in the kitchen to make myself some warm milk. I thought I heard you in here talking to someone." She walked over to my closet and looked in. "You're not hiding anybody, are you? You know the rules about having friends stay over—you're supposed to check with me first."

"Nobody's here—honest. I must have been talking in my sleep. I guess I heard you coming and woke up."

She frowned. "I know what I heard," she said. "And I heard two voices." She walked to the bed and picked up Nicholas's hat. "What's this?" she asked.

I took it from her. "It's—ah—it's a hat."

"I can see that. Where did it come from? And why is it all wet?"

"It's part of a costume—for school. But it got dirty, and I wanted to wash it." That had to be one of the lamest stories I had ever come up with, but I guess the Dumpster believed me. At least she didn't ask any

64

more questions. Instead, she looked under the bed and then around the room.

Suddenly her hand flew to her mouth and her eyes opened wide. "Oh, no!"

I wheeled around, sure that Nicholas was back and ready to bean her with a snowball, but I couldn't see anything. "What's the matter?" I asked.

"Just look at the mess in here," she said, picking up a soggy sock with two fingers. "You clean this up tomorrow, Iggy Sands. If your father found out I let you live like a pig, he'd fire me in a minute."

I stretched, gave out a big yawn, and rubbed my eyes. "Tomorrow, Dottie. Honest—I'll clean tomorrow. But it's so late, and I'm so tired." I yawned again.

She must have felt sorry for me. She came over, wrapped her arms around me, and gave me a big hug. "You're cold," she said. "Let me make you some warm milk. Or hot chocolate."

"I just want to go to bed. But thanks anyway."

When she left, I made sure my door was closed tight. I waited until all the kitchen noises were quiet. Then I whispered, "Okay—you can come out now." When nothing happened, I whispered a little louder, "She's gone. Come on. I want to talk to you." I paused for a few seconds. "I need some advice."

But nothing happened. I concentrated hard, trying to make him appear. Still nothing. I saw the book lying on the floor. I closed my eyes and said, *"Shun gad, shun gad, shun gad."* When I opened my eyes, there he was.

"Where'd you go?" I asked.

"You didn't want her to see me, did you?"

"Does that mean other people can see you? Besides me, I mean?"

He shrugged his shoulders.

"Look," I said, annoyed, "if you're not going to answer my questions, why do you keep popping back?"

"I told you—you called me. I don't know why I'm here, and I guess you don't, either. But you'll figure it out. Call me when you do. I'll come—provided you *really* need me. You're a pretty smart guy—when you stop to think about what you're doing. And if you don't want me, don't call."

"But I still don't understand—" I started to say when, suddenly, he was gone.

"You forgot your hat!" I yelled toward the place where he had been. But he didn't come back, and I sure wasn't going to *shun gad* him back. I rolled the hat under my bed. If he wanted it, he'd find it.

One thing for sure—I didn't need a ghost in my life who knew less than I did and thought it was funny to throw snowballs at me in the middle of the night. I picked up the book, shoved it back into the silver box, and stuffed it into the bottom of my underwear drawer.

CHAPTER

11

I decided not to tell Ed and Drool about Nicholas. They probably wouldn't believe me. And besides, if Nicholas was going to help anybody, I wanted it to be me—*if* I ever got desperate enough to call him again.

On Monday I heard Dr. Harder tell Mr. Humphrey that they'd better keep an eye on me, so I guess she still didn't trust me. Simon was walking around acting like he was already elected because his dumb tag sale had raised $89.32—big deal! And Dee and I had to announce our activities to Dr. Harder by Friday. I didn't know what I could come up with.

On Tuesday I was headed toward the cafeteria with Drool and Ed when Caitlen popped up out of no-where and stood in front of us. She was dressed in designer jeans and a silk shirt and looked just short of fantastic.

"Hi, Iggy," she said. "Mind if I walk to the caf with you guys?"

I was about to say *Of course not,* when Ed said, "Yeah—we mind." He turned to me. "Don't we, Iggy?"

My cheeks were hot. Of course I didn't mind Caitlen hanging around. But I did have my reputation to worry about, especially with Ed and Drool right there. Why couldn't she have asked me when I was by myself?

Suddenly they were all looking at me, waiting for me to say something. I took a deep breath. "Sorry, Caitlen, but we have a meeting—some campaign strategy to talk about. Maybe some other time, okay?" I kept my eyes on her, trying to read a reaction. Would she believe me? I also didn't want to look at Drool and Ed, who, I knew, were giving me dirty looks.

"Yeah, okay. Some other time," she said.

As she walked away, Ed gave me a punch in the arm. "Are you nuts? What do you mean, 'Some other time'? Why didn't you tell her to get lost?"

"Yeah," Drool added. "What's she up to, anyway? How come she's so interested in you all of a sudden?"

Maybe because she thinks I'm a pretty sharp guy, I thought. But I wouldn't say it out loud. "She's okay," was what I finally did say.

"Okay?" Ed hollered. "Have you lost your mind? She's a snob. She walks around like she doesn't want to breathe the same air we do. And you're telling us she's *okay?* What's the matter with you, Iggy?"

I walked into the caf with the two of them right on my heels, going on and on about me getting soft and losing my mind. We had reached the end of the hot lunch line when Ed called me stupid, and I wheeled around. "That's enough," I said. "I told you before, I'll tell you again—don't *ever* call me stupid. And get something else straight—Caitlen is Dee's best friend. Maybe we could learn something from her—about what Dee's doing in her campaign."

Ed started shaking his head. "There you go again—acting like this campaign stuff is for real. You've got to be stu ... nuts to think you've got a chance. And in the meantime, if I didn't know you better, I'd think you were in love."

Drool laughed—a spitting, spluttering laugh. "That's it. You're in love. You look at her with those puppy dog eyes. Next thing we know, you'll be writing your initials and hers inside hearts."

Drool was still laughing, but Ed's eyes had turned to slits and he was studying me. Ed was my friend, but he had a fiendish mind. If I wasn't careful, there'd be red hearts plastered all over the school announcing I was in love with Caitlen. I definitely didn't want that to happen.

"You're wrong," I said, putting a cool edge to my voice. "Both of you. And I'll prove it to you. Next time I see Caitlen alone—you just watch what I do."

I got an order of hamburger and fries, and as I started walking toward our usual table, Ed said, "Do it now."

"Do what now?"

"Whatever you're going to do to Caitlen," he said. "She's sitting all by herself, at that table in the corner."

I looked to where he was pointing. Sure enough,

there was Caitlen, all alone. And to make it even worse, she was looking right at me—and smiling.

"This isn't a good time," I said to Ed.

"Yeah—right. Whatever." He gave me such a look of disgust that I felt like I had turned into a geek or something.

And then Drool had to add his two cents into it. "I'm telling you, Ed. He's in love."

That was it. I took my tray and walked over to where Caitlen was sitting. But I didn't sit down right away. I don't know—it was like I was expecting her to tell me to take a walk or something.

She looked up and flashed me her fabulous smile. "Iggy! Hi."

That smile made me feel like I could rule the world. "Is this seat taken?" I asked, trying to sound casual. But I didn't wait for an answer before sitting down.

She was impressed—I could tell.

"So, Caitlen. How come you're here all alone? Where's Dee? And all your other friends?"

She leaned in so close to me that I could smell her hair—like flowers in spring. My head was spinning so fast that it was hard to concentrate on what she was saying. Something about a fight, and how she'd never talk to Dee again as long as she lived. When she put a hand on my arm, I thought it would burn through my shirt.

And then, from two tables away, I heard a loud "Ahem!" and a couple of phony coughs. I lifted my eyes and saw Ed and Drool giving me the evil eye. It was time to make a quick decision—did I want Caitlen? Or did I want the friendship of Ed and Drool?

When I realized what Ed could do to my reputation, I also realized there was no choice. Not really.

I stiffened. Caitlen was chattering away about everything and nothing. I caught Ed's eye and, making sure Caitlen didn't see, gave him a thumbs-up sign.

"I think Dee's looking for you," I said to Caitlen, looking over her shoulder toward the door. As she turned around to see, I grabbed two of the longest french fries on my tray, dipped them heavily in ketchup, and shoved them up my nose.

"I don't see—" she started to say. But then she looked at me, looked at the french fries hanging out of my nose with ketchup dripping from the ends, and looked like she wanted to throw up.

And as I sat there, doing a poor imitation of Dracula with my fang fries, she stood up, turned around, and walked toward the other side of the caf.

Drool and Ed came running over. "That was fantastic, Iggy," Drool said. He grabbed two fries, dunked them in ketchup, and shoved them in his ears. "Try this one next time."

Ed was doing one of his snort laughs. He could hardly talk. "Did you see her face? Did you? She'll never bother us again, you can bet on that." He slapped me on the back. "You haven't lost your touch. I had my doubts there for a while, but you're still the best."

I pulled the fries out of my nose and wrapped them in a napkin. Drool pulled the fry out of his right ear and started to nibble on the ketchup end. "Don't eat that," I said, grabbing the fry out of his hand.

"Why not? It's a perfectly good french fry."

71

"But it's been in your ear. It's probably got ear wax all over it."

"No, it doesn't," he said, pulling out the other one and examining it. He took a bite. "Besides, I'm only eating the end with the ketchup on it."

I couldn't watch. What did I care about Drool's eating habits anyway? I turned to Ed. "So, are you satisfied? I told you that Caitlen didn't mean anything to me. I was just waiting for the right opportunity."

"I'll never doubt you again, Iggy, old buddy. Now— when are we going to start making plans? For Operation Sabotage, part two? I keep waiting to hear what your brilliant scheme is."

"Soon, Ed. Just be patient."

He was about to start asking more questions when Drool reached over and grabbed a handful of fries off my tray. "If you're not going to eat these, I will. I hate to see good food go to waste."

"Help yourself. I'm not very hungry. And listen," I said, pushing my rolled-up napkin in his direction. "There's two more wrapped up—in case you want them."

He started to reach for the napkin. Then he started to laugh, bits of chewed-up potatoes spewing from his mouth. "You're a riot, Iggy. They're your nose potatoes. I can't eat those."

I didn't even answer.

The bell rang, ending lunch, and as I walked out the door I spotted Caitlen. She was still by herself, and she looked lonely. But I knew that she'd probably never talk to me again.

CHAPTER

12

When I got home, the Dumpster was pulling hot brownies out of the oven. Her headphones were going full blast, but when she saw me, she turned down the volume and took them off. "Iggy? Are you all right?" she asked. "You look like you lost your best friend."

"Not quite," I said, plopping into a chair. "But almost."

She put a glass of milk and a warm brownie in front of me. "Eat. You'll feel better."

I pushed the plate away. "Thanks anyway, Dottie. I'm not hungry."

She sat down next to me. "That bad, huh? Want to talk about it? Does it have something to do with a girl?"

I looked at her and frowned. "Who said anything about a girl?"

"I don't know. Just something about that look on your face."

When I didn't say anything, she said, "Sometimes, when you're having problems with someone, it's best to clear the air. And if you did have an argument with someone—I'm not saying it's a girl, mind you—but if it was, you should call her."

I shook my head. The idea of calling Caitlen was making me break into a sweat. "I couldn't do that."

"Why not?"

"I wouldn't have anything to say."

She laughed. "You, Iggy? Not have anything to say? She must be someone pretty special."

I stood up. "Besides, the way I feel has nothing to do with a girl."

"Whatever you say," she said. "I'll leave the brownies here in case you get hungry later."

I walked into my room. What if I called her? What if she hung up on me? What if I apologized before she did?

I didn't think I could call, but I looked up her number in the phone book. I picked up the phone. I felt a lump in my stomach, like I had eaten a whole onion pizza. I dialed her number. One ring—two—three—

"Hello," a voice said. I knew right away—it was Caitlen.

"Hello. Caitlen?" Two words. That was about all I could manage. The lump in my stomach was working its way up to my throat.

Silence. Two seconds that felt like two hours. And then—"Iggy? Is that you?"

I couldn't believe it. She didn't hang up. Not yet, anyway. And she recognized my voice. My turn to say something.

But I didn't have to. "I'm so glad you called," she said. "I wanted to call you, but I didn't have the nerve. I hope you'll forgive me for walking away from you like that. It was so rude. I'm really sorry. But when you said Dee was coming in, I didn't want to see her. She makes me so mad. That's why I had to get out of there. You're not mad at me, are you?"

"Me? Mad at you?" My voice was squeaky, so I stopped talking.

"Iggy? Are you still there?"

I cleared my throat again. In my deepest and smoothest voice I said, "I'm here, Caitlen. And I'm not mad at you. I mean, I was—but I'm not." Then I ran out of words again. "I—ah—just called to—" I cut my words off. I should have planned this better. I knew she was waiting for sparkling conversation, and I was having trouble with simple sentences. "I wondered about the homework—whether Mrs. Phister gave us any math homework for tomorrow."

"Iggy, we had tons—and I mean tons." She giggled. "Didn't you write the assignment down?"

"No—I mean, sure I did. But I left my homework notebook in school. Would you mind telling me?"

"Not at all," she said. And as she read off the page numbers and the problem numbers, all I could think of was that she had a great voice. "Did you get it all?" she finally asked. "I didn't go too fast, did I?"

"No, I heard every word you said." And of course I didn't write it down. I never did much homework—just enough to get by.

"By the way, Iggy," she said. "Did you decide what you're doing for your campaign project? It's due by

75

the end of the week, you know." She hesitated a minute. "Unless you don't want to tell me—"

"Of course I want to tell you," I said quickly. "But I haven't decided yet. But you'll be the first to know— if you want to be."

"I know how clever you are, that's all," she said. And she laughed one of her golden laughs.

And then there was nothing else to talk about. When I got off the phone, I felt like I was in shock. It was hard to believe she hadn't noticed the fries hanging out of my nose, but why would she pretend she didn't if she did? I could feel myself smile. Maybe Caitlen really liked me.

Suddenly I was starved. The smell of brownies had worked its way into my room. The Dumpster was okay. What I liked most about her was the way she could give answers without asking a lot of questions— and she baked the best brownies in the world.

During math the next day Mrs. Phister decided to come around to each of us and check homework. I was always good at bluffing, but there was Caitlen, sitting right next to me, watching. I couldn't say I didn't have the assignment because I didn't want Caitlen to think I was a liar. But I didn't want her to think I was stupid, either.

"I'm sure it's here somewhere, Mrs. Phister. It took me almost all night to do it." I kept ruffling through the pages of my notebook, pretending to be upset that I couldn't find what I was looking for.

"Well, Mr. Sands?" Mrs. Phister's voice came out

like ice. "I'm waiting. Did you or did you not do the math assignment?"

"Of course I did it. I told you, it took me hours." I closed my notebook and looked up at her. Even under pressure like this, I could be cold, too. "I must have left it home. I'll bring it to you tomorrow. Will that be okay?"

She sighed. "I guess it will have to be."

As she turned to walk away, I relaxed. But she stopped abruptly, turned, and looked at me over her glasses. I could sense trouble.

"By the way, Iggy," she said, tapping her pen on her open grade book, "I see that you still owe me a math test. You never made up the one you missed, and grades will be closing soon." Her pen started tapping faster as she said, "That test will make a big difference in your grade. You'll have to get a B-minus to get your name placed on the election ballot, Mr. President."

Her mouth was smiling at me, but her eyes weren't. I knew she didn't want me to get elected. She didn't trust me any more than Dr. Harder did.

I leaned back in my seat and smiled back at her. "No sweat, Mrs. Phister. I'll ace that test."

"Good," she said. "Tomorrow. After school." And she turned to check the next kid's homework.

After school I was hanging around the front door, thinking maybe I could say hi to Caitlen, when Ed and Drool came over. As I talked to them, my eyes traveled around.

"You coming with us, Iggy?" Drool asked. "We're going over to the Sundae School for ice cream."

"I don't know," I said. "I should be getting home."

Ed made a face. "What for? You never rushed home before. How come all of a sudden you're busy all the time?"

I thought about the math test I should try to study for and the homework I had to make up. Suddenly I caught sight of Caitlen out of the corner of my eye. She was walking alone, and when she saw me, she slowed down.

I guess I was staring at her, because all of a sudden Ed said, "What's the matter with you, Iggy?" He turned, saw Caitlen, and frowned. "You're turning to mush, Iggy. But if you'd rather stay here and talk to a girl, that's fine with us."

They started to walk away. Caitlen looked up, smiled, and waved. I realized I wouldn't know what to say to her. Cheeks flushing, I waved quickly back and ran to catch up with Ed and Drool.

CHAPTER

13

The Sundae School is a favorite hangout for kids of all ages. It has the best ice cream sundaes in town, and out back is a little farm with ducks, a couple of pigs, and a cow. Lots of kids like to feed the ducks, but not me. My favorite is the cow. Everybody says her name is Bossie, but I call her Flops—because that's what she spends most of her day doing.

After we stuffed ourselves on hot fudge sundaes, Drool bought himself a big bag of chips, and we walked around the farm for a while. We were leaning over the fence watching Flops chew on her tongue when Ed asked me the same question he always asked.

"So what's going on with this president thing, Iggy? You going to pull something off soon or what?"

"Yeah," I said, not taking my eyes off Flops. "I'm going to pull something off."

"You planning to tell us?" Drool asked. He had

79

eaten his way halfway through the bag of chips, but more were on his shirt and on the ground than had made it into his mouth. A couple of ducks were pecking at the ground around him.

"Yup," I said. "I am. And I guess there's no better time than right now." A few more ducks had flocked around, and they were fighting over pieces of potato chips. "Let's go sit up on that rock, and I'll outline my whole plan to you." As we walked away, the squawking ducks started to follow.

Ed grabbed the bag of chips out of Drool's hand, dumped what was left in a pile on the ground, and threw the empty bag away.

"Hey!" Drool hollered. "What'd you do that for?" He gave Ed a shove.

Ed shoved him back. "I don't feel like being in the middle of some stupid duck fight. You've got lousy eating habits, Drool."

Drool stood there, spluttering, trying to think of a good insult.

As I started to walk away, I looked back and said, "If you two morons are interested in hearing my plan, you'd better hurry up. Because I don't feel like wasting my time watching you—or the ducks—fight over potato chips."

We climbed to the top of the rock and sat down. I took a deep breath, gathering up my thoughts. They didn't say anything—just sat there with their faces looking like big question marks.

"My plan is simple. I'm going to win the election."

Silence. Stone dead, absolute silence. They looked at me. Drool's mouth was hanging slightly open with potato chip crumbs on his bottom lip. Ed's mouth was a thin, tight line. I waited, listening to the ducks squawking, to the sounds of kids yelling and playing, to the wind blowing dry leaves.

Finally, looking like he was struggling with a tough math problem, Drool asked, "Why?"

Ed just kept looking at me. Then the tight mouth turned into a slight grin. "Oh, I get it. It's a joke, huh?"

"No," I said, my voice cold and serious. "It's not a joke. Just think about it. If I could win—if I could become president—we could have a blast. Not just for a couple of months, not just for a campaign, but for a whole year."

"I don't know about you," Drool said, "but this campaign hasn't been much of a blast. All we've done is worked on Simon's tag sale, and that was boring—"

"And we've spent a lot of time waiting for you to come up with some dynamite plan to mess up the school," Ed interrupted.

That's when I grinned. Ed had fallen right into my trap. "And what better way to mess up a school than to make Iggy Sands president?" I asked. "The teachers will freak. And so will Dr. Harder." I looked from Drool to Ed. I couldn't tell what they were thinking. I wasn't sure they *were* thinking. "So what do you say? Are you in this with me?"

Drool was the first to answer. "I guess so, Iggy. But if you win, can you make me your vice-president?"

"I'll certainly try." I turned to Ed. "And you? Can we count on you?"

He still had that serious look on his face. "I don't know...."

I stood up and looked down at him. "You could be treasurer. You could be the one to handle the money. Decide how we spend it. What kinds of trips we go on." I wasn't sure if that's what the treasurer did, but it sounded good to me. And it must have sounded pretty good to Ed, too, because he stood. Then, quietly, he said, "Ed Witbread—Treasurer." He looked at me and nodded. "I like the sound of that. Think you could arrange it?"

"Not if I don't get elected, I can't." I wasn't sure I could arrange it even if I did get elected, but I couldn't worry about that now.

He put his arm around my shoulder. "Well, so what's next, Mr. President? What do we have to do now?"

I knew he was hooked. "We have to come up with a class activity—some kind of fund-raiser."

"Like what?" Drool asked. "Simon's tag sale was boring. And I'm not getting into some dumb bake sale or car wash."

"Me, neither," I said. "We'll have to think up something really great—something that'll get all the kids excited." We jumped off the rock and walked back to where Flops was. She had walked over to the fence and was still chewing.

Drool patted her head and said, "Sometimes I think it would have been easier to be born a cow."

Ed slapped Drool off the head. "Didn't anyone ever tell you? You were."

Drool gave him a shove. "No, really. Look at that

cow. All she has to do is eat, sleep, and swish away the flies with her tail."

"Yeah, and create great big stinky cow flops," I said, laughing. Because that's exactly what Flops was doing—taking a big dump. And she didn't even care that we were standing there watching her.

That's when it hit me—one of my all-time great ideas. "Splotto!" I yelled. "That's our fund-raiser—Splotto!"

"What are you talking about?" Drool asked.

"I read about it—in some magazine. This school ran a lottery. They divided their field at school into squares, and they sold each square. Then they got a cow and let her wander around. Whoever owned the square where she took the first flop won."

I could see Ed and Drool grinning as I told them about the plan. "We sell chances on cow flop?" Ed asked.

"You think the teachers would let us do something like that?" Drool asked.

"I don't see why not," I said. "Other schools have done it. I'll find the article and show it to them. It's a great idea. We'll raise all kinds of money, and everyone will get a big laugh out of it. But whatever you do, don't talk to anyone—and I mean *anyone*—about this. Until I announce the idea on Friday, it has to be our secret."

As we walked away working out our Splotto plan, Ed slapped me on the back. "You know what, Iggy? I'm going to enjoy being your treasurer."

CHAPTER

14.

When I got home, I opened my math book. I tried to study—I really did. But the problems didn't make sense and the numbers jumped around and the answers were never the same. I'd need a miracle to pass that test and get that homework done.

That's when I remembered Nicholas—he said he'd come if I really needed him. Anyone who could pluck snowballs out of the air shouldn't have any problem making me a math genius.

I did the *shun gad* routine, and sure enough—there he was.

"What happened to you?" I asked. He was a mess—all dirty and muddy and smelling like a swamp. "Don't they have showers where you come from?"

He gave me a disgusted look and didn't answer. I was afraid he'd leave in a huff, so I said, "I decided to give you another chance. I have a problem. A big one."

"I hope it's important," he said, slightly out of breath. "I was busy—frog hunting." He made a fist and held it near my face. At first I thought he was going to punch me, but he turned his hand over and opened it. A large green frog with buggy yellow eyes sat in his hand right in front of my nose. The frog opened his mouth and let out a croak that sounded like a burp. I stepped back from the swampy smell of frog breath.

Before I could say anything, Nicholas said, "Tell us your problem. We'll do what we can." The frog hopped onto Nicholas's shoulder and sat there, looking at me.

"We? What do you mean, *we?* You mean you and that frog?"

"Be careful what you say," he whispered. "Frogs can have powers you never dreamed of."

I didn't want to mess with magic frogs, so I said, "It's math. If I want to run for student council president, I have to do a pile of homework. And I have to do really well on a makeup test after school tomorrow. I don't know where to start." I stopped talking, waiting for him—or his frog—to zap me smart.

He just looked at me. "So?"

"So—I figured you could help me—make me smart so I can do word problems and all."

He laughed. "Me? You want *me* to help with math? I hate math." The frog let out another croak.

What a joke! I could call up a ghost anytime I needed him, and he hated math. "I don't get it," I said. "What good was all that magic? What good is it making you appear and putting up with you and your

85

smelly frog if you can't even help me with my homework?"

He answered with another question. "Who's the best math student in your class?"

I thought for a minute. "Simon—Simon Ackmar. He's the smartest kid in everything—except common sense and personality. He's a real stiff."

"Then he's out. Who else is good in math? Someone you respect."

I thought again. Nicholas must have a way of tapping into another kid's brain, so I wanted to choose carefully. "Murphy—Murphy Darinzo."

"Then there's your answer. Call him up and ask him for a quick math tutoring session."

"That's it? That's your great solution? Call someone up and *study?*"

"You have a better idea?"

"No, but you'd better come up with something else," I said. "I can't ask Murphy for help. He called me a jerk."

"How come?"

I told him about the shaving cream bomb and Murphy's project that got ruined. "It was just a joke, but he won't talk to me until I apologize, and I never apologize."

He shook his head. "You *are* a jerk." The frog croaked as if it was agreeing with him.

I was starting to burn. "I don't have to take this from you, Nicholas. Or from your frog. You smell—both of you."

"So, you like jokes, do you?" he asked. As he talked, he started pointing to spots on the floor. Frogs started popping up everywhere until almost the whole floor was covered with the buggy-eyed green things.

"Hey!" I yelled over the noise of croaking, burping frogs. "You can't do that."

"I already did," he said. He touched my shoulder. When I turned to look, a frog was looking back at me, his frog lips moving in and out inches from my face. I was too surprised to say a word.

"You know why you're a jerk?" Nicholas asked. "Because you're letting your pride get in the way of what you want, that's why. And if you don't want to hear the truth about yourself, don't call me—it's up to you, you know."

And then he was gone, and so were the frogs. All except the one that was still perched on my shoulder, croaking in my ear. "Hey!" I yelled. "You forgot your frog." I lifted it off my shoulder and looked at it. Maybe there was a beautiful girl under that ugly green body, waiting to be kissed. The idea made me laugh. Too bad—she'd have to wait a long, long time. I opened my window and watched the frog hop away.

I picked up the phone and dialed. Maybe Nicholas was right—maybe I was being stubborn. And maybe I did owe Murphy an apology.

When he answered the phone, I said, "Hi, Murphy? This is Iggy. You know how I said I never apologize? Well, I was wrong. I'm sorry about your project. I'll find a way to make it up to you."

"Thanks, Iggy," he said. I could tell that he was pleased. "You have to admit—it was pretty childish."

Don't push it, I thought.

"Listen," he continued. "If you ever need any

help—with your campaign or anything—let me know."

Perfect. He was an okay guy. "As a matter of fact," I said, "I am having a little problem with math. Do you think you could help me out?"

"Sure," he said. "I'm not busy now. Why don't you come over?"

By the next morning I was ready. I had done all the homework I had to give Mrs. Phister, and after a two-hour tutoring session with Murphy, I knew I could breeze through the test.

But when lunchtime rolled around, I started to get nervous again. I was walking into the caf when I stopped short. Drool, a step behind, bumped right into me. "Hey!" he hollered, as another kid collided into him. "What are you doing, Iggy?"

"I forgot something," I said, heading back toward the classroom. "Don't wait for me."

I sat on the floor in the corner of the room and started looking over the chapter the test would be on when I heard the door open. I was dead—Drool and Ed would never stop teasing me when they found out I'd skipped lunch to study math. I slammed my book shut and shoved it behind my back.

But it wasn't Drool and Ed—it was Caitlen.

She walked toward her desk and started looking for something when she spotted me. "Iggy," she said, sounding surprised. "I didn't know you were here." When she saw me sitting on the floor, she asked, "Are you all right?"

I stood up and brushed myself off. "I'm fine. I just

came back to look for—uh—to—" I couldn't think up an excuse for being there.

But I guess I didn't need one, because she started talking—about Dee and how she didn't care if she never talked to her again. "She thinks she's so smart. I heard her telling someone about her plan for a class activity, and it really stinks—a combination car wash–bake sale. Did you ever hear anything so uncreative?" She gave one of her little laughs.

I laughed along with her. "It sounds pretty bad," I said.

"I'll bet you came up with something fantastic. You have such a clever mind."

"Actually, it's kind of ordinary," I said. I didn't know why, but I was feeling a little shy. I didn't want her to think my idea was silly.

She laughed again. "There's *nothing* ordinary about you, Iggy Sands. Won't you tell me your plan?" Then her mouth turned down. "Unless you don't want to."

"Of course I want to," I said quickly. And I told her all about Flops and Splotto, making her smile and giggle with delight.

"You're amazing, Iggy Sands. Do you know that?" she said when I was finished.

Then the bell rang, and I knew the class would be coming back. I didn't want to get caught in there alone talking to Caitlen, so I made a quick excuse, grabbed my math book, and headed for the boys' room. I hadn't gotten much studying done, but my time hadn't been wasted.

When I got back to the room, everyone was quiet

and sitting down, and Mrs. Phister looked mad. As I passed Drool's desk, I whispered, "What's going on?"

He looked up at me and grinned. "The food fight," he whispered loudly. "As if you didn't know."

He started to chuckle when Mrs. Phister said, "I told you, I want absolute silence." She looked at me. "And where—exactly—have you been, Mr. Sands?"

"I just came from the boys' room, Mrs. Phister. I didn't go to lunch today."

"Is that so? Well, we'll just have to see—" she started to say when the P.A. crackled and Dr. Harder's voice pushed into the room.

"Boys and girls, I want every one of you to pay close attention," she said. "What happened in the lunchroom today was a disgrace." She paused for a minute. Drool turned around, caught my eye, and gave me a thumbs-up sign. Ed looked over and gave one of his snorting laughs.

Mrs. Phister walked over to Ed, and he changed his laugh to a cough and slumped down in his seat.

Then Dr. Harder's voice came back. "Since many of you seem unable to control yourselves, starting tomorrow, all seats in the cafeteria will be assigned. You will be walked to lunch by your teachers. The lunch line will be closely monitored. And you will not—and I repeat, *not*—be allowed to leave your seats for any reason until the bell rings and you are escorted back to your classrooms. Any student who is not in his or her seat once lunch begins will be severely disciplined. This will continue until the student responsible confesses."

As soon as she stopped talking, everyone started to

complain. "It's not fair." "It'll be like a prison." "It's the only time we get to talk to our friends." Mrs. Phister shushed us again, and then looked at me as if I had something to do with it.

When school was over, I stayed in my seat, ready for my test. Mrs. Phister was busy at her desk and didn't seem to notice me at first. When I coughed, she looked up, puzzled. "Yes, Iggy? Is there something you want to tell me?" She hesitated a minute and then added, "Speak up—confession is good for the soul, you know."

"I'm here to take my math test, Mrs. Phister. I was in here studying all through lunch." The look she gave me said I might as well try to tell her I walked on the moon during lunch. But she fumbled around in her desk, pulled out a sheet of paper, and said, "Sit right in front of my desk, please." Her trust in me must have been somewhere around minus ten.

I struggled through the test—and I mean struggled. It was hard, but I didn't give up. I wasn't going to let Mrs. Phister—or math—keep me off the ballot for president.

When I got home, Drool called. He talked nonstop about the food fight and how it had to be one of the best pranks I had ever pulled off in my life. I tried to tell him I couldn't take credit, but he wouldn't believe me. He kept calling me modest.

As soon as he hung up, Ed called. He wasn't quite as excited about it as Drool, but almost. Then came the hardest question of all: "What are you going to do about Dr. Harder's new rule?"

"What do you mean?" I asked.

"You know, about how we can't get out of our seats during lunch. All the kids were talking about it after school, but Drool and I told them not to worry. We told them you'd come up with something. Because of your leadership and all. I figured it was good for your campaign."

I couldn't believe it. I hadn't done anything, and I certainly didn't want to do anything now to get in trouble. "Ed," I said. "Listen to me. I know you don't believe me, but I had nothing to do with the food fight—honest. And I can prove it. I have an airtight alibi."

He was quiet for a minute—thinking, probably. Then he said, "Oh, yeah? What is it?"

I thought about being in the room with Caitlen the whole time the food fight was happening. I thought about how she could prove I was nowhere near the cafeteria. I thought about what Ed would say if he knew what I had been doing. "It's a long story," I finally said. "I don't want to go into it now."

I thought Ed would get mad, but he didn't. Instead, he said, "That's okay, Iggy. If you think of something by tomorrow, let us know. If not, we'll understand. Sometimes even great people run out of ideas. You'll still make a good president."

CHAPTER

15

I got to school the next morning about fifteen minutes early. I didn't hang around waiting for Ed and Drool—I went right into class. I was hoping Mrs. Phister would have my test grade for me.

She was sitting at her desk—right where I had left her the afternoon before.

I flashed her my best smile. "Good morning, Mrs. Phister. How are you feeling?"

She looked up and frowned, and I had to work hard to keep smiling. Pushing her glasses back up her nose, she said, "I just finished grading your makeup exam."

I didn't like the way she sounded, but I kept smiling. "Did I do okay?"

She started tapping her fingers on the desk. "It was a very difficult test," she said and paused.

As if I didn't know that—but I didn't say anything.

"Makeup tests are always harder," she continued.

"They have to be. Students taking makeups have more time to study."

So get to the point, I thought. My neck was starting to sweat, and all of a sudden I knew I hadn't done well. The test was going to ruin me.

Still looking at me, she turned a paper over. I knew it was my test—I could tell from the handwriting—but she had her hand over the top where the grade was. "Quite frankly, Iggy, I didn't expect you to do very well. But this grade—"

I was in a panic. She pulled her hand away. And there—in red pencil—89. I couldn't believe it. I had come close to getting an A on the hardest test I had ever taken in my whole life. I started to punch the air and let out a big holler when I caught Mrs. Phister's expression. I pulled my arm to my side. "Is there something wrong?" I asked.

She was looking past me, and I turned, thinking someone had come in. But no one was there. She started to talk, but I had the odd feeling it wasn't to me. "It's just that—with a test of this difficulty—but you were sitting right in front of me—I don't know how . . ."

She let her voice trail off. But I knew what she meant. She thought I cheated. She didn't think I could pass the test. And she was probably disappointed, because now my grade couldn't keep me off the ballot. Well, too bad, Mrs. Phister.

I flashed another smile and reached for the test. "Can I take this home? I want to show my father when he gets back."

She handed me the test and smiled slightly but didn't say anything.

I took my test and turned to leave. I had done so well, but for some reason I was feeling like someone's dirty sock.

I was at the door when she called me back. Maybe she wanted to apologize for making me feel so lousy. But she handed me another sheet of paper and said, "While you're here, you might want to check your new lunch assignment. You'll be at table number eight, seat number five."

I looked at the list. My table was packed with people I either didn't know or didn't like. And seated right next to me was Simon Ackmar. "I can't eat at this table," I said. "Couldn't you put me at a table with at least one of my friends?"

She raised an eyebrow and pulled the list out of my hand. "I think you should consider yourself fortunate to be allowed in the cafeteria at all. Just remember Dr. Harder's rule—no one out of seats—for any reason. Anyone breaking that rule will have all privileges taken away—the entire faculty has agreed to that."

It didn't take a genius to figure out what she meant. They didn't want to take a chance that I might become president.

As I left the room, I couldn't stop thinking about Dr. Harder's stupid rule, and all of a sudden I knew exactly how to start the perfect protest—without anyone breaking her rule.

I found Ed and Drool, pulled them into a corner, and explained my plan. I knew it was a good one, because Drool was panting and saying, "Yeah, yeah,

yeah," and Ed was laughing and snorting so much I thought he'd choke.

"There's just one thing," I said. "I can't be involved. Dr. Harder and the teachers are all waiting for me to do something—anything—so they can have an excuse to drop my name from the ballot. I'll have to count on both of you to spread the word. Tell only people you trust. And tell them to wait for the signal—when Simon Ackmar stands up."

"How are you going to manage that?" Ed asked.

"Trust me," I said.

We slapped each other a few fives, and they hurried off to get things started.

Right after the national anthem, Dr. Harder came on the P.A. and repeated her new rule. Then Mrs. Phister made a big deal about handing each of us a card with a table number and a seat number printed on it. When she was finished, she said, "I'm just sorry that the guilty party did not come forward. And because of that, we all have to be punished." I figured she was looking at me, but I was busy. I had propped a book open on my desk so she couldn't see the rubber cement I was spreading on the top of my notebook. As it dried, I rolled it into tiny balls and dropped them all in a plastic bag.

When the bell rang for us to go to lunch, Mrs. Phister said, "Form a line single file at the door. We will not leave until everyone is quiet."

Ed was ahead of me in line. I leaned forward and whispered, "You got enough kids?"

"Plenty," he whispered back. He was about to say

more, but Mrs. Phister swooped down on us like a hawk, and we stood quietly at attention.

As we walked toward the cafeteria, lines of other kids came down the hall—all so straight and quiet that I felt like we were in a prison camp. A few kids, as they saw me, smiled briefly or nodded, then quickly looked away. The only sounds were the shuffling of feet and an occasional cough, but I felt like there was electricity charging through the air.

We went through the doors, lined up for hot lunch or milk, and headed for the tables and chairs we had been assigned. On each table was a number, and on each orange plastic chair was taped a card with a seat number in black marker. No one had any excuse for sitting in the wrong spot.

I took my seat between Simon and a girl named Kate. As I sat down, Simon looked at me like I hadn't showered in a week. I gave him the famous Iggy smile, and he turned back to his lunch—spaghetti topped with a smooth red sauce, shiny salad, and bread.

I had never heard the cafeteria so quiet. I checked the clock. We were ten minutes into lunch. Perfect.

I reached into my pocket, pulled out my bag of rubber cement balls, and emptied them into my hands. Holding my hands near my nose, I sniffed once. Twice—a little louder.

Simon turned toward me to say something. I threw my head back—then forward. The sneeze that exploded from me was a masterpiece, and as I sneezed, I turned slightly toward Simon's lunch and let the little rubber cement balls spatter all over his lunch and all over him.

He bolted out of his chair saying, "Ohh—grosssss! That's disgusting."

At the same time kids all over the cafeteria grabbed their orange plastic chairs and, holding them under themselves, started walking around the cafeteria. A couple stopped, sat for a minute with friends, then stood up—with their chairs—and started walking around again. Within minutes it seemed like most of the kids in the caf were holding on to their chairs and walking around.

The teachers went nuts. "What are you doing?" Mrs. Phister shouted. "Get back in your seats!" yelled Mr. Humphrey.

I never moved. And neither did Simon. He stood there, brushing himself all over. His spaghetti looked like it had turned into a lumpy meat sauce with my sneeze, and little dark balls covered his salad, his bread, and his tray.

Dr. Harder came rushing in with Mr. Bussey, the gym teacher, right behind her. He shoved his silver whistle into his mouth and blew. Everyone froze.

Very slowly and very quietly she said, "I *demand* an explanation." Her eyes traveled around the room, looking for a victim. It was like Russian roulette— wherever those eyes stopped, the kid would have to talk. She settled her gaze on Murphy Darinzo and Peter Patterson. "Murphy? Peter? Whatever would possess you to disobey my rule? It was made quite clear."

Murphy, still holding his chair in a half crouch, said, "But we didn't disobey your rule."

Dr. Harder's eyes became narrow slits. "You were told to stay at your assigned table."

"No, we weren't," Peter said. "Your rule was that no one was to leave his or her assigned seat."

"And we didn't," Murphy added.

Ashley Douglas, who had carried her chair to another table, said, "The only one who left his seat was Simon—and he's still out of it right now."

All eyes turned to Simon. He turned bright red. "It was just ... I mean, Iggy sneezed and ... he made me ..." His voice trailed off.

Dr. Harder turned to Mr. Humphrey. "When did this start?"

Mr. Humphrey scratched his chin. "I'm not sure. Everything was fine until"—he looked toward Simon—"until Simon stood up. Then everyone started to move."

"Simon, come with me," Dr. Harder said. "And the rest of you—" She slowly shook her head. "Just finish your lunches. Sit wherever you want. But behave yourselves."

As she left with Simon, a huge cheer went up in the cafeteria. Drool and Ed came over and sat with me. They were congratulating each other on our success, but I wasn't paying attention. My mind was already on the meeting with Dr. Harder after school. Once I announced my plans for Splotto, I knew I could roll into the office of president.

CHAPTER

16

As I rushed to Dr. Harder's office after school, I thought about how exciting my Splotto idea was. It would be the best activity to hit Westford Elementary—ever.

Mrs. Phister and Mr. Humphrey were both at the meeting with Dr. Harder. Simon was the last to arrive. There was an empty seat next to me, but he picked it up and moved it off to the side. "I'm more comfortable over here," he said. "Besides, I already did my activity. I'm only here to listen."

"Suit yourself," Dr. Harder said. I couldn't decide if she was mad at Simon or not—maybe she thought he had something to do with the cafeteria protest. One thing for sure, she wasn't acting like he was Mr. Perfect anymore.

She straightened some papers on her desk, picked up a pen, and said, "Let's begin. Which of you would like to go first?"

I wanted to go first, but I decided my idea would sound even better after Dee's car wash–bake sale plan. "Ladies before gentlemen," I said and smiled.

Dee looked at me, jacking a big phony smile up on her face. "Why, thank you, Iggy. I always knew you were a gentleman." She turned toward Dr. Harder and the teachers. "It's a simple idea," she said. "And even though it might sound a little strange, I think it'll be tons of fun. Lots of schools are doing it. The activity is called Splotto, and all we need is a cow and the ball field. I have outlined my whole plan." And she passed a couple of typed pages to Dr. Harder.

It was like I had been slapped in the face. I stood up, knocking my chair over. Everyone stared at me. "That's *my* activity," I said. "I thought of it first. You stole it."

Dee just sat there, looking up at me. She didn't say a word at first. Then she turned to Dr. Harder and said, "I don't know what he's talking about. I read about Splotto in a magazine."

Dr. Harder looked from Dee to me. "You've made a severe accusation, Ignatius. Do you have any proof?"

"Of course I do," I said, my voice sounding like I was strangling. "I told all my friends about it—a couple of days ago."

"All your friends?" Dee said. "We're talking about Ed Witbread and Drool Haygood here, aren't we?"

Dr. Harder leaned forward. "We'll need more proof than your two friends. Did you tell anyone else?"

"Yes, as a matter of fact, I did," I said, my mind in a fog. "I told—" I was about to say *Caitlen* when

101

the fog cleared. Caitlen—who had said she hated Dee. Caitlen—who was suddenly so nice to me. Caitlen—who listened and laughed as I told her my whole plan. What I jerk I'd been. I shut my mouth—tight—and sat down.

Dee sat back and folded her arms. "You didn't tell *anyone,*" she said, biting off her words. "You're just jealous because Splotto is a fabulous idea and you want to steal it." She turned back to Dr. Harder and the other teachers. "Now that that's settled, would you like to hear all about Splotto?"

Dr. Harder sighed and shook her head. She looked tired. "Yes, Dee, by all means. Continue."

I barely listened, but I heard enough to know that every single bit of my Splotto plan was coming out of Dee's mouth—right down to where she'd get the cow.

When she was done, Dr. Harder smiled and said, "It's very interesting. And if, as you say, other schools have done it, perhaps we could consider it." Then she turned to me and said, "We'll hear your idea next, Ignatius."

"That *was* my idea," I said. "I don't have another one."

Simon spoke for the first time. "If Iggy doesn't have an activity planned, he shouldn't be allowed to run. Today was the deadline, you know."

Dr. Harder cleared her throat. "Yes, Simon, we do know." She leaned forward and looked at me. "I suppose it *might* have been possible for both candidates to come up with a similar idea. It's not *probable,* but it is *possible.* Therefore, if Mrs. Phister and Mr. Humphrey agree, I am willing to give Ignatius a small extension of time to present his idea."

Both teachers nodded slightly, and Dr. Harder continued. "You'll have to get your act together by Monday, Ignatius—that's when we announce the activities to the school—or we'll have no choice but to drop your name from the ballot."

As we walked out of the office, Drool and Ed met me in the hall. "So?" Ed asked. "How did it go?"

I was so mad I couldn't talk. I watched as Dee bopped down the hall. Caitlen was waiting for her, and I knew Dee was telling her what had happened because they both started squealing and laughing and hugging.

As they walked toward us, laughing and talking, I wanted the floor to open up and swallow me. "Hey, Iggy," Caitlen called in her sweetest voice. "I hear the Burger Factory is having a sale on nose fries—extra long for extra big noses."

They hurried off. Their giggles seemed to echo off the walls as anger and embarrassment burned through me.

"What was that all about?" Drool asked.

"Nothing," I said, hardly able to talk.

"So tell us what Dr. Harder thought of Splotto," Ed said.

"I guess she liked it. But it's not my activity—it's Dee's. She stole it right out from under me and told them about it first. Dr. Harder gave me until Monday to come in with an activity."

Ed glared at Drool, who said quickly, "Don't look at me. I didn't tell anyone—just like Iggy said. Honest!" Then he pointed at Ed and said, "Maybe *you* opened your big mouth."

They were going to get into a big fight over it, so I stepped between them. "Look. Forget it. It's not important. Besides, I should have listened to you guys in the first place."

"What do you mean?" Ed asked.

"I mean I'm withdrawing. I'm taking my name out. I never wanted to run for president anyway. It was a stupid idea."

"You mean you're quitting?" Drool asked.

"You got it," I said.

"You can't," they both said together.

"You'll be a great president," Ed said.

Drool grinned, his cheeks turning red. "And I'll be a great vice-president. And Ed's already got some ideas about being treasurer."

I looked at Ed. "You do?"

His cheeks started to turn red, too—it was the first time I had ever seen Ed blush. "Don't quit, Iggy," he said. "Not yet anyway. Splotto was a dumb idea. Let Dee have it. You'll come up with something better—I know you will." When I didn't answer, he added, "At least think about it, okay?"

It was all crazy, and I wanted to walk right into Dr. Harder's office and quit. "There's no guarantee either of you will win the elections in the fall, you know."

"We know that," Drool said. "But if you're not president, we don't even have a chance at a chance . . ."

"Or a hope of a hope," Ed added. "You have all weekend. You'll think of something."

And I figured it didn't make much difference if I quit right then or if I quit Monday, so I said okay. But I knew there was no way I could come up with anything better than Splotto.

I spent the weekend trying to come up with a better idea, but the more I thought, the less my brain worked. As I was leaving for school Monday morning, my head still empty, I asked the Dumpster, "What was the best activity you ever had when you went to school? For a fund-raiser, I mean?"

"That's easy," she said. "Every year we had a talent show. The kids all loved it—being up there onstage. And all our friends and families came. The school always raised a ton of money."

"No kidding. Did you ever win?"

"No, but I came in second once. I was quite a tap dancer in my time." All of a sudden she started dancing and singing—loud.

"You're pretty good, Dottie," I said as I left. "You should have won."

By the time I got to school, the idea of a talent show didn't seem too bad. When I told Dr. Harder about it, she said, "I actually like it much better than Splotto." That got me worried. If Dr. Harder thought it was a great idea, the kids would probably hate it. Maybe I should have checked it out with Ed and Drool first, but it was too late now.

The assembly was right before lunch. Dee went first. She outlined her Splotto idea, and the kids went wild. They laughed and cheered and stomped, and I knew everyone would be buying a patch of ground, hoping it would get flopped on first.

Then it was my turn. I walked to the podium and adjusted the microphone. I could see Caitlen sitting in the front row watching me. No smile now. Ed and Drool were about three rows behind her, leaning forward and waiting to hear my plan. I could tell that they expected something spectacular.

I cleared my throat. "Dee's idea of Splotto is very interesting," I began. "Whoever thought it up must be very clever." I looked right at Caitlen, but she turned her head.

"But I think my idea will raise more money. What I propose is ..." I paused to add a little drama "... an all-school talent show. Everyone loves the stage, and this will be your chance to perform."

I didn't expect wild applause, but I didn't expect the dead silence that followed, either. Ed and Drool slumped down in their seats, and I heard some moans and groans. I was dying up there, and everyone knew it. My hands were getting cold and my feet were starting to sweat. But my brain was working overtime.

"I know that may not sound like much," I said. "But you haven't heard the best part."

Everybody quieted down, and Drool and Ed sat up again. I wasn't quite sure where I was headed, but I knew it had to be good.

"Not only will there be a talent show for you and for your family, but the winner is going to get a fabulous prize."

Someone in the audience shouted, "Oh, yeah? What?"

"First prize will be . . ." Will be what? What would these kids want more than anything? What would I want? I took a deep breath, and before I knew what I was saying, the words were coming out of my mouth. "First prize will be four tickets to the Crusty Crew's summer concert in New York City."

And this time the applause *was* wild. Kids whistled and cheered. I raised my arms to quiet them down. They were putty in my hands. "We'll charge admission. You can sell tickets to your family and friends. Come up with the best act, and you'll be sitting at the Crew's concert."

Right after the curtain closed, Dr. Harder came over to me. "Ignatius, was that wise? The school can't afford those concert tickets—even if we could get them."

Dee had a smirk on her face. "You really did it this time, Iggy—lying to the whole school." Simon was right behind her, nodding and looking pleased.

"It wasn't a lie," I said. "My dad gave me those tickets. I have them at home. I'll bring them in tomorrow and show them to you."

Dr. Harder looked so happy I thought she'd do a cartwheel. "That's so very generous of you, Ignatius. Donating those tickets to the school." She put her arm around my shoulder and gave me a squeeze.

Simon started grumbling, ". . . it's not fair . . . it's just not right . . ." and Dee stuck her nose in the air and stomped off.

As I left the auditorium, kids kept coming up to

me, slapping me on the back, and telling me how great my idea was. Even Ed and Drool started talking about the kind of act they could put on.

But I wasn't feeling great—the last thing I wanted to do was give those tickets away. I knew what I had to do—I had to be the winner of that talent contest.

CHAPTER

17

I needed help—big time—so I decided to call on Nicholas. I must have said *shun gad* a hundred times before he finally showed up. He hadn't done anything for me yet, so I figured he owed me.

"Now what?" he asked when he arrived. At least he wasn't all muddy and smelly.

I told him what had happened. "So *do* something," I said. "Something besides just talking or fooling around. What I need is action."

He started to lift his arm. I could just see him zapping up a roomful of snakes or a tornado or something. "Wait—don't!" I yelled, my arms covering my head.

He scratched his head. "Don't what? Why are you so jumpy?"

"I don't know. I just want you to help me win the talent show."

"Sure. Do you want me to teach you how to tap dance?"

I could just see me tippity-tapping onstage with everybody laughing hysterically. "No, thanks," I said. "I already know what I'm going to do—a magic act. I got a magic set from my father for my birthday last year, and he brings me home tricks that I've added to it. I'm pretty good."

"Then you don't need me," he said.

"Yes, I do. The routine I do is okay, but it's nothing spectacular. For my grand finale, I want to do a disappearing act."

He pulled back. "How are you going to manage that?"

"With your help. I'll put myself into a big box and close the lid. Two seconds later you pop up at the back of the auditorium, dressed just like me, and let everybody see you. They'll think it's me. Then, two seconds later, you disappear, and I pop back out of the box. Isn't that a great idea?"

"Isn't that cheating?"

"Magic doesn't have any rules."

"Life does. People have to follow certain rules. Otherwise you can get yourself into big trouble."

"But you don't seem to follow any rules."

"I never did. If I did, I probably wouldn't be—" He stopped talking and was staring at the wall.

"Wouldn't be what? A ghost? Is that what you mean? You never do hang around long enough to tell me about yourself."

"I don't like talking about myself. I don't think of myself as a ghost. I'm more like . . . a spirit."

"What's the difference?"

"Oh, a lot. Ghosts don't seem to know they're

dead—they're too serious. They go floating around haunting old houses and scaring people. I was old when I died. But I decided to hang around afterward and help people—at least for a little while."

I frowned. "You haven't been much help to me. And what do you mean you were old? You're not old now."

"That's what I like about being a spirit. I can be any age I want. It all depends on who I'm helping. I'm kind of enjoying being a kid again."

"So does that mean you'll help me?" I asked. "You said that's why you're here. Come on, Nicholas. You haven't done anything great for me yet. You're a ghost—or a spirit—or whatever you call yourself. You pop in and out. I could use that."

He paced around for a minute. I held my breath. Finally he said, "I'll tell you what—I'll try."

"Try? What do you mean, *try?* Why can't you just promise me?"

He shook his head. "I can't explain it. I haven't been this young in ... in a long time. Sometimes it's hard to control myself. You must know what I mean."

"I guess so. But that's okay. I know you'll come through for me. Now—want to see some of my magic? It's not as good as your snowballs or your frogs, but with the disappearing act, I know I can win."

Nicholas sat on the bed. He looked a lot like me when I was trying hard to be serious and not fool around.

The tricks were stored in a big black box that I used as a table. I pushed it into the middle of the room and did a couple of tricks. Flowers popped out of nowhere, and I pulled a rabbit—fake, of course—out of the plastic top hat that came with the kit.

"What do you think?" I asked as I put the hat on and took a bow.

"Not bad," he said. "Not great—but not bad."

"What was wrong with it?"

"I don't know. What else can you do?"

I thought for a minute. "I can juggle. It took me almost a year to learn, and nobody knows I can do it. Watch this." I took three beanbags from the kit, took a deep breath, and started them going.

Nicholas watched for a minute, then yawned. I tossed the bags higher to make it more exciting. All of a sudden he got a funny little grin on his face. He pointed toward the bags, I lost my concentration, and they fell—one on the floor, one on my head, and one on my shoulder. It took no more than a second to realize what Nicholas had done—he had turned my beanbags into eggs, and one had broken on my head and was slithering down my face.

Nicholas was holding his sides, laughing.

I was furious. "You can't do this to me," I hollered. And I grabbed the egg that had broken on my shoulder and threw it at him.

That's when my father walked in. "Surprise—I'm home ..." He stopped his sentence in midair. "Iggy? What's going on in here? I thought I heard someone laughing. And someone else yelling."

I looked toward my bed. Nicholas was gone—of course.

"I guess I'm not much of a magician," I said. I felt

the egg yolk ooze past my ear and plop on my shoulder.

He looked puzzled. "What are you doing?" he asked.

"Juggling," I said. "Or trying to."

"With *eggs?* Why?"

I didn't know what to say. I sure wasn't going to mention Nicholas. My father would think I was nuts. "It's kind of a long story," I said, trying to smile.

He shook his head and smiled back. "Why don't you get cleaned up and then tell me what this is all about."

It was good to have Dad home. Talking to him on the phone for a couple of minutes every night wasn't as good as talking to him in person. After I showered, we sat in my room as I gave him all the details about running for president and Splotto and the talent show and my great idea about doing a magician's act. "I need a really great act—I have to win." Maybe with Dad's help, I wouldn't need Nicholas.

"It takes years and a lot of equipment to create a complicated act," he said. "But we could work on a simple routine. It'll be a good act, but I can't guarantee a winner."

"You don't understand," I said. "I *have* to win."

He looked puzzled. "I understand that you want to win the election," he said. "But will winning the talent show make that much of a difference?"

I turned away from him. "Remember the tickets you gave me to the Crusty Crew?" I took a deep breath and, all in a rush, said, "Well, I was onstage explaining my idea, and all the kids seemed to hate

113

it, and I felt like I was dying up there, so I told them there was a terrific first prize, only I didn't really have one, and that's when I . . ."

I stopped to catch my breath. As I turned to face him and tell him the rest, he smiled at me and said, "And you offered your tickets as the prize. I can understand how that happened. The stage can be a very frightening place—especially if you feel like you're losing your audience."

"Did it ever happen to you?"

The smile faded. "What do you mean?"

"I found the trunk in the attic—the one with your scrapbook in it. You were famous, weren't you? And Mom was your assistant. How come you gave it all up? Is that why she left?"

He sighed. "I never talked much about my past to you. But I told myself when you were old enough, I'd explain everything. Is this a good time?"

"It's a very good time," I said. "Why don't you tell me now."

He leaned back. "When I was young—right out of high school—I became a magician's assistant. He taught me a lot of his tricks, and I was pretty good. After he retired, I took over his act. I enjoyed traveling all over, performing in front of people. I met your mother in my travels, and she became my assistant. We fell in love—at least we thought it was love—and got married. Then you were born, and I wanted to settle down and raise a family. But your mother loved traveling, loved performing, loved the excitement of crowds—all the things I had gotten tired of. We decided it would be best if we went our separate ways."

"Do you ever hear from her? Do you know where she is?"

"Still traveling. Still performing. She sends a postcard about twice a year."

"I didn't know that. How come you never showed me?"

"I wasn't sure you'd understand. Maybe I was afraid you'd want to be with her—instead of with me."

"Why would I want to do that?"

He shifted in the chair. "I don't know. Maybe you'd think your life would be more exciting with your mother."

I laughed. "Believe me, Dad. My life is plenty exciting. Tell me more about your act. Could you teach me some tricks? Could you show me how to make somebody appear or disappear?"

"How much time do you have to get this act ready?" he asked.

"About a week."

"Then let's stick to rabbits out of hats," he said and laughed. "It'll take more than a week to have you master a disappearing act, okay?"

"I guess so," I said, but I remembered what Nicholas said. That he'd try. I was hoping he'd try real hard.

CHAPTER

18

I did more things that week than I thought were possible. I got Murphy to help me organize the talent show and Mr. Humphrey to agree to be the master of ceremonies. I practiced my magic act and my juggling act with Dad as my audience. I needed some kind of a magician's outfit, so I found a big piece of black material and made a cape. I polished the black plastic top hat from my magic kit. I made a sign for my act: IGGY THE MAGNIFICENT. And I did all my homework and studied. What I didn't do was call Nicholas. I wanted to save him for my act.

On Saturday I had to go to Splotto. I didn't want to, but if I didn't show up, I'd be breaking the campaign rules. It seemed like the whole town was there, hoping Flops would lay a big one on their patch of ground. It took a couple of hours, but when she finally flopped, Simon turned out to be the winner. I was hoping that was all he'd win this year.

Dee saw me and strolled over. "Wasn't this absolutely the *best* idea?" she said, her voice dripping like honey. "Too bad you didn't think of it first. It made s-o-o-o much money. Lots more than your talent show will, I'll bet."

I could feel the blood rushing to my face. When I spoke, my voice was tight and quiet. "Just remember something, Dee Kruse. You might have fooled a lot of people into believing this was your idea, but you know and I know where you got it. Your soggy brain couldn't come up with an idea, so you stole mine."

She jammed her hands on her hips and stuck her face in mine. "Oh, yeah? Prove it," she said, practically spitting in my face.

We stood there, glaring at each other, when Dr. Harder came over. She was carrying a shovel and a plastic bag. "Oh, Dee, there you are," she said.

Dee unlocked her eyes from mine and faced Dr. Harder with her big phony smile. "Wasn't my Splotto idea a big success? Did we make a ton of money?"

"I would say so," Dr. Harder said. Then she handed Dee the shovel and the bag. "I thought you might need these."

Dee looked confused. "What for, Dr. Harder?"

"To clean up the field, of course," Dr. Harder answered. "We certainly can't leave cow flop lying around, can we? And it seems the cow left quite a few more piles after she deposited her first one, so make sure you get them all."

"But—but—but—" Dee was starting to sputter and her face looked a little green. "I can't do this."

"Of course you can," Dr. Harder said. "Maybe one of your friends will help you." And she walked away.

Dee stood there, holding the shovel and the bag. I patted her arm and smiled. "This might be the beginning of a wonderful career for you, Dee." By the look on her face, I knew she wanted to take a swing at me, but her hands were full, so she stuck her nose in the air and stomped off. "See you tomorrow afternoon at the talent show," I called after her. "Maybe you could do an act with your bag and shovel."

Sunday morning Dad gave me some last-minute hints as I rehearsed my act one last time. "Will you come to the show?" I asked, putting my hat and props into the big cardboard box I planned to use for the finale.

"I wouldn't miss it for all the world," he said. "You are about to become 'Iggy the Magnificent' and carry on a long family tradition. I'm very proud of you."

"Were there more magicians in our family?" I asked.

"There sure were. Your great-great-grandfather was 'Sandovich the Magnificent.' That was in Russia, a long time ago. He grew up in the court of the czar and became the court magician. I understand he had a reputation for being a practical joker as a child—and a rebel as he got older. He didn't like to be told what to do. His stubbornness sometimes got him into trouble."

"Why? What happened to him?"

"I'm not sure. But I've heard that when a man named Rasputin became friendly with the czar and his

118

wife, your great-great-grandfather Sandovich didn't trust him. And I guess Rasputin didn't care for him, either, because he turned the czar against him. Anyway, there was a legend in the family that Sandovich disappeared right in the middle of one of his acts and was never seen again. I don't know if it's true. But I guess he was quite a character."

I wasn't sure why, but I was getting goose bumps.

He looked at his watch. "You'd better hurry. Mrs. Haygood will be here in a few minutes. I have to run a few errands, but I'll see you at the show," he said and hurried out. Drool's mother was giving me a ride. Drool and Ed had worked up a comedy routine, and everyone in their families was going to watch.

I folded up my cape and put it into the box. Then, at the last minute, I pulled the silver box out of my drawer and put it in the box with the rest of the stuff. Nicholas was somehow connected to the box, and I wanted to make sure he'd show up when I needed him.

When we got to the school, the parking lot was starting to fill up. That was a good sign because I was hoping for a big audience. Twenty-three kids had signed up to perform, and all their friends and relatives wanted to see them.

As we went backstage, Drool said, "Me and Ed are on fifth, Iggy. Want to come and watch the other acts with us?"

"No, you go ahead," I said. "I'll catch up with you later."

The first thing I did was find Mr. Humphrey. "Everything's under control," he said. "And I put you on last, just like you asked."

"Thanks," I said. "And listen. When you introduce me, tell the audience that I'm doing a genuine disappearing act for my finale."

He raised his eyebrows. "No kidding?"

"No kidding. It's going to be a showstopper."

I dragged my box of stuff into one of the small closets backstage that the school used as a dressing room. On the door I taped a sign that said IGGY THE MAGNIFICENT—PRIVATE—KEEP OUT! I pulled my hat and cape out of the box, put them on, and looked in the mirror. Not bad. The hat was a little shiny and the cape was a little short, but I looked pretty good.

As I practiced my tricks in front of the mirror, I could hear the show going on. When Drool and Ed started their comedy routine, I opened the door a crack to listen. I could hear the audience laughing, but Drool and Ed's jokes were so bad that I wondered if the audience was laughing at *them*. Oh, well, I was sure it wouldn't matter to Ed and Drool—as long as they could get a laugh.

When their act was over, I knew it was time to call on Nicholas. I took a deep breath and said, *"Shun gad, shun gad, shun gad."*

Nothing.

I tried a few more times.

Still nothing.

"Come on, Nicholas," I said out loud. "This is no time to play games. You *promised* me." I closed my eyes tight and said the chant again very slowly. I felt a breeze. But when I opened my eyes, it was still just me and my reflection in that room.

Why wouldn't he come? Then I thought, "Maybe because we're in a different place. Maybe *shun gad* isn't enough. Maybe he needs the whole chant again, like we did the first time."

I opened the silver box. But the book was gone. There was nothing in the box but a piece of folded-up paper.

Hands shaking, I opened it and read, "Sorry—I got hung up. Might be late—might not make it at all. But that's okay—there's magic everywhere. Just learn how to use it."

I stared at the paper. I was so mad I wanted to scream. "Thanks a lot, Nicholas," I said out loud. "Thanks a whole big lot!" I crumpled up the paper, shoved it into the silver box, and slammed the lid shut. Then I took off my hat and cape, rolled them into a ball, and tossed them back into the cardboard box. I might as well forget it—forget the act, forget the show, forget the election.

Suddenly someone tapped on the door. Nicholas—it had to be. It was all one of his bad jokes. As I pulled the door open, I said, "You have some nerve—" and saw my father standing there, holding a big box.

He looked puzzled. "Murphy said you might be back here." Then he looked around. "Who has some nerve? Is something the matter? Are you ready? Two more acts and you're on."

"I'm not doing it," I said.

"What are you talking about?"

"I'm not going on that stage. I'm not doing the act. You came here for nothing."

He put his box on top of my cardboard box and took the cover off. "Everyone gets nervous before a performance." He reached into the box. "I thought you could use this," he said, shaking out a heavy black satin cape with a bright red lining. He put it around my shoulders and hooked the collar together. "And this . . ." he continued, reaching back into the box and pulling out a black top hat—a real one, with black sequins on the hatband—and a shiny black magic wand. He put the hat on my head, handed me the wand, and turned me around to look in the mirror.

I adjusted the hat. "They're amazing!" I said.

He smiled. "They were mine. I had them packed up in the attic. I thought it was time to pass them on to my son—Iggy the Magnificent. Are you ready?"

And that's when I knew that I had to go on. Even if it meant without Nicholas—even if I lost the talent show—I couldn't let my father down. "I'm ready," I said. "Could you help me with my props?"

As we took the stuff out of my cardboard box, he picked up the silver box. "Where did this old thing come from?" he asked. "I haven't seen this for years."

"I found it—up in the attic. I thought there might be a treasure in it."

He laughed. "I used to think so, too. It was passed down from that great-great-grandfather I was telling you about. The Sandovich who disappeared. But I could never figure out how to open it. My guess is— it's empty."

I could hear the act before mine ending, and I knew I had to hurry. "Dad?" I asked. "My great-great-grandfather—Sandovich the Magnificent—would you know what his first name was?"

"Sure," he said. "Nicholas. Nicholas Ignatius Sandovich."

CHAPTER

19

As I waited backstage listening to Mr. Humphrey announce my act, I had the feeling I was forgetting something.

"Ladies and gentlemen and children of all ages—for our final act, we have that great magician, Iggy the Magnificent. He will amaze you with his tricks."

I was about to step onstage when he added, "And tonight, as a very special surprise, he will perform— before your very eyes—a disappearing act." Uh-oh— that's what I forgot—to tell him I wouldn't be disappearing. My father gave me a puzzled look, but I just smiled and shrugged.

I walked out and took a bow. Dad's hat and cape made me feel like a pro, and I loved the spotlight and the applause. Every trick I did worked perfectly—I made flowers appear from a rolled-up newspaper and then disappear again. I made a hoop float in the air. I juggled. I pulled a rabbit out of a hat.

When the act was over, the audience clapped politely. I knew what they were waiting for—they were waiting for me to disappear.

I took a deep breath. In a loud voice I said, "And now—ladies and gentlemen—Iggy the Magnificent will disappear before your very eyes." I swished my cape around me, bowed, and walked offstage.

It was quiet for about thirty seconds. Then they all started to laugh and applaud. "Encore!" someone yelled, so I went back onstage and took another bow.

As I walked offstage, my dad met me and said, "You were wonderful. I'm so proud of you. And where did you get that *disappearing act* idea? It was a riot."

"Just a last-minute idea," I said. "Was I good enough to win, do you think?"

He didn't answer, because just then Dr. Harder walked onstage and took the microphone. "The judges tell me they had a very hard time deciding on a winner. And because the voting was so close, we are going to award two prizes. As you all know, the winner will get four tickets to the Crusty Crew concert—thanks to Iggy Sands, who was the brains behind this afternoon's show. And the runner-up will get a gift certificate for a pizza party and a free movie rental."

She fixed her glasses, cleared her throat, and said, "The runner-up in tonight's talent show is—Iggy the Magnificent!" My heart sank. Free pizza and a movie, and someone else was going to be rocking with the Crusty Crew. Dr. Harder looked in my direction and whispered loudly, "Iggy?"

I looked up at my father, who patted my shoulder and then gave me a gentle push. I took the gift certificate from Dr. Harder, thanked her, and was about to leave when she said, "Stay here, Iggy, while I announce the winning act." She had her arm clamped around my shoulder, so I didn't have much choice.

"And the act that won first place—just by one vote—is *The Twinky Twins!*" While I was trying to figure out what she was talking about, Caitlen and Dee, dressed like two giant Twinkies, walked onstage. My head was swimming as they took *my* concert tickets from Dr. Harder and bowed. Everybody in the audience stood up and cheered. I knew the show was a big success, but I felt like a loser.

After the show Drool's father asked if Dad and I wanted to go out for pizza with Drool's and Ed's families. But I wasn't hungry. I took off my top hat and cape. They could go right back up into the attic—I wouldn't be needing them again.

Dad and I didn't say much on the ride home—he must have guessed I was feeling lousy. "Were they good?" I asked as we pulled into the driveway. "Dee and Caitlen—were they really better than me?"

He rubbed his chin, thinking. "I don't think they were better. Just different. Their song-and-dance number was okay, but their costumes made the act. Maybe that's why they won." He reached over and ruffled my hair. "I know how disappointed you are. But don't be. Your show was a success and so was your magic act. Did you enjoy it? Performing in front of all those people?"

I thought about being up there on the stage, hearing

126

the audience cheer, and having the spotlight on me. "Yes," I finally said, feeling a smile creep over my face. "I guess I did. I mean—up there, all alone—with no one to count on but me—I really felt like somebody."

"That's what's important," he said. "That's what life is all about—finding out what makes you happy, finding the magic—there's magic everywhere. You can't always expect to win, but you have to learn to believe in yourself."

What he said made me gasp. "What do you mean, *'There's magic everywhere'?"*

He got a kind of faraway look in his eye. "Someone said it to me a long time ago—I can't even remember who. Maybe it was in a dream. But I've never forgotten it. *Magic everywhere?* I guess that means friends and family and doing a good job. It's gotten me through a lot of tough times."

I had a million questions to ask him, but for some reason, I didn't want the answers—not right now, at least. "I'm kind of hungry," I said.

"Me, too," he said and laughed. "How about we shake this gloomy mood and go get some pizza with the guys?"

"On one condition," I said, reaching into the back seat. "I get to wear your hat."

"It's *your* hat, Iggy the Magnificent."

First thing Monday morning, Dr. Harder came over the P.A. to announce the results of the weekend activities. I held my breath as she said, "These two activities raised an enormous amount of money for our student activities fund." And then she announced the totals. Splotto had raised ten dollars more than the talent show.

I slumped down in my seat as Dee, two rows over, cackled and said, "Twice a loser, Iggy. With number three coming up on Friday." She was talking about the election. We had four more days before the whole school would vote for a new president for next year. Caitlen, next to me, didn't say anything. She just sat there with a smug grin plastered on her ugly face.

When it was time for recess, Ed and Drool told me to wait for them outside—they had something to do. Just when I was ready to go looking for them, they showed up. "Where were you guys?" I asked.

Instead of answering my question, Drool said, "Don't let Dee get to you—she's just a snot."

"Yeah," Ed chimed in. "Maybe she won the talent show dressed up like a giant snack, but she won't win the election."

"Don't be so sure," I said. "She's been doing some big-time campaigning. She's got her name on posters plastered all over the school."

"Big deal," Ed said. "Come on—we want to show you something." They looked around to make sure Mrs. Phister wasn't watching, then pulled me into the building.

"Hurry up," Drool said, pulling at my T-shirt.

I was about to knock his hand off when he stopped and pointed. Posters and signs were hung all over the walls—and they all had my name on them.

I looked at Ed and Drool, not knowing what to say.

"Well?" Ed asked. "What do you think? We

worked on them all weekend. My whole family helped."

"Mine, too," Drool added.

I shook my head. "You guys are unbelievable." And right then and there I knew it didn't matter if I won the election or not. What mattered was that I had two of the greatest friends in the whole world.

CHAPTER
20

What a week it was. Simon, Dee, and I campaigned like mad. We shook hands and talked to kids before and after school. We handed out flyers. Ed and Drool wrote IGGY THE MAGNIFICENT FOR PRESIDENT on every blackboard in colored chalk. The lettering looked so good that Mrs. Phister didn't erase it. She worked her math problems around it.

By Friday morning, the day of the election, I was exhausted. My voice was hoarse, my hands were sore, and my face felt frozen in a permanent smile. Running for president was no easy job.

Right after the national anthem, Dr. Harder came on the P.A. "As you all know, today is election day. Your teachers will be handing out ballots in a few minutes. Vote carefully. We need a president who will work hard. Someone with a good head on his or her shoulders. Being president is a big responsibility." And the P.A. clicked off.

I almost felt like she was sending the silent message "Don't vote for Iggy Sands."

Suddenly Dee stood up. "Remember, everybody. *Responsibility* rhymes with *Dee*. So you know who to vote for."

Mrs. Phister looked at her sharply. "The campaigning is over, Dee. Now sit down."

Dee's cheeks turned red, and she quickly sat down. But as soon as Mrs. Phister turned her back, Dee looked over at me, pointed to herself, and mouthed the words "I'm a winner." I had a hard time staying in my seat and keeping my mouth shut, but I did.

Mrs. Phister handed out the ballots. "As soon as you vote," she said, "fold your ballots in half. I'm coming around with a box for you to put them in."

The rest of the day dragged by. Every time I looked at the clock, I was sure the hands were stuck. Everything we did was in slow motion—math, reading, spelling, even recess. At lunch I sat with Ed and Drool at a corner table, but I couldn't help seeing all the kids who seemed to want to talk to Dee. Miss Popularity. Whatever made me think I could beat her?

Finally—finally—the end of the day crept around. Fifteen minutes before the last bell, Dr. Harder came on the P.A. "And now, the news you've all been waiting for—the announcement of our new student council president." Then she paused. I could feel my body breaking into a cold sweat.

She continued. "We have never, in the history of Westford, had such a close election. All three candidates are to be congratulated for their hard work and ambitious campaigns."

Come on, I thought. *Get this over with.*

"We recounted the votes three times because the candidates were within ten votes of one another." She paused again. Ten votes. *Dee beat me by ten dollars in the activity. Don't tell me it's going to happen again.*

I dropped my head down and squeezed my eyes shut as Dr. Harder said, "The winner—by just ten votes—is Iggy Sands!"

There was a moment of absolute silence. I sat there, frozen, as everybody started to go crazy. Ed and Drool jumped out of their seats and danced around, slapping each other high fives. Dee stood up, jammed her hands on her hips, and said, "It can't be. It can't be. I want those votes counted again. There's been a mistake." Mrs. Phister looked like someone had nailed her shoes to the floor.

Murphy was the first one to come over to me. "Nice going, Iggy," he said. "How's it feel to be president?"

"I don't know," I said, grinning. "A little scary."

"If you need any help, you know you can count on me," he said.

Then the final bell rang, and the kids started to crowd for the door. Dee was the first one out, and I figured she was headed for Dr. Harder to complain. Caitlen looked at me and was about to say something when Ed and Drool came over. "Let's go celebrate," Ed said. "We have to talk about this treasurer thing."

"Yeah," Drool added. "And about the vice-presidency."

Caitlen gathered up her books, put her head down, and left.

When I got home, I couldn't wait to tell Dad the

good news. But he wasn't home yet, so I went in my room. I wanted to tell somebody—somebody who didn't know—and the only one I could think of was Nicholas. I sat on my bed and closed my eyes. *"Shun gad, shun gad, shun gad,"* I said out loud and waited.

Suddenly the phone rang. Nicholas—it had to be. I picked it up on the second ring. "Nicholas? Is that you?"

"No, it's Caitlen," the voice said. "Iggy, are you still mad at me?" Her voice was soft and sad.

When I didn't answer, she said, "I just wanted to congratulate you. I knew you'd win. You'll make a great president."

It was hard to be mad at her. "Thanks," I said.

"I know you probably won't believe this, but I told a lot of kids to vote for you. I knew you'd be better than Dee."

I took a deep breath. I wasn't going to let her sweet-talk me again.

"And another thing," she continued. "About those Crusty Crew tickets? I was thinking—maybe you'd like to go with me. I mean—you don't have to tell me right now. You can let me know. But I think we'd have a good time. And maybe we could talk about me being your vice-president. You'll have a lot to say about the office, and I'd really like that. I could help you out—a lot—if you know what I mean."

I was having trouble thinking. I should trust Caitlen about as much as I should trust a cobra. But she was asking me to go to the Crew concert. I reached under the bed, pulled out Nicholas's hat, and put it on. I knew that from now on, whatever I did was going to

133

be up to me. And right now I didn't want to make any quick decisions.

I heard Caitlen say, "Iggy? Are you still there?"

"I'm here, Caitlen," I said, rubbing the hat. "And I'll tell you what—I'll have to get back to you. But when I decide something, you'll be the first to know." And I hung up the phone.

One thing I knew for sure—Westford Elementary would never be the same after a year of Iggy the Magnificent as president.

About the Author

M. M. RAGZ is the writing coordinator for Stamford High School in Stamford, Connecticut. She literally does her writing on the run, developing story ideas while jogging five miles a day. While her job with the school system keeps her busy teaching writing, conducting writing workshops and seminars, and giving book talks, Mrs. Ragz occupies her free time with a range of activities that include watercolor painting, crafts, gardening, and summers on Cape Cod in Eastham. She holds three college degrees from the University of Connecticut and Fairfield University. She has traveled to Germany, Mexico, Greece, Britain, and the Caribbean.

She lives in Trumbull, Connecticut, with her husband, Phil, and their youngest son, Michael, who is the inspiration for many of Murphy's adventures. All of her books about Murphy and Murphy's friends, *Eyeballs for Breakfast, Eyeballs for Lunch, French Fries Up Your Nose, Sewer Soup,* and *Stiff Competition,* are available from Minstrel Books.